INDEX

Dedication 2

Prologue 3

Preface 5

Introduction 6

Chapter I: The True Doctrine 8

Holy spirit symbology and its meaning 13

The fruit of the Holy Spirit 16

The Gifts of the Holy Spirit 24

The ministries 33

Chapter II: Nimrod and Semiramis, the Beginnings of Idolatry 41

The ankh 51

The demonic principalities of nimrod, semiramis and the leviathan 58

Chapter III: God's People and the Idols 63

The diverse forms of idolatry 63

Anathema Symbols we should avoid 74

Chapter V: Origins of some festivities 109

Chapter VI: Deceptions of the Enemy and some prophetic fulfillment 116

Conclusion 143

References 146

Dedication

With pleasure I dedicate this work to all youth. I also dedicate this work to all adults and the elderly consecrated to Christ. It is my deep desire and feel God bless you richly and abundantly.

Prologue

Since the downfall of mankind, by trying to fill the emptiness that they undoubtedly have, and by the enemy's influences, have sought to whom and what to worship. In their furtive search and ironically, has worshiped from lifeless things to even animals and pagan deities, among other things.

God has created man in His image and likeness. He has made him superior to other living beings with abilities not shared by any other being created by God: only he can repent of his sins and submit to Christ. Only he was given the blessing of being able to start a new life, after having fallen.

In this search, man has come across with the enemy of souls, and by offering his soul was seeking, answers and things that only God can give: the liberation and salvation of the soul.

It's good to know the enemy's traps, and to know that he has subordinates anchored to the shores of the spiritual paths with the sole intention of distracting and confusing you; he offers spiritual substitutes to "fill you up" for a moment, but in reality he is offering you a placebo that will captivate your soul and will lead you to eternal darkness (this was the case of Simon the Magician; Acts 8:9-24)

When the Lord sent the seventy, he said to them: "Carry neither purse, nor scrip, nor shoes: and salute no man by the way" (Luke 10:4). We can understand that he told them: 'Do not be distracted by the path, do not let anyone deviate you from the commission you were given'. A distraction in our walk with the Lord can cost us very dearly. Distraction means driving away the attention from the thing that was applied (in 2 Romans 4:29 we find the same principle). In a distraction the enemy can play us a nasty move (in this he is an expert), and lose our lives, and the saddest part is that this life is not just physical! But the greatest dilemma and the greatest concern is that your eternal life is at stake.

This book is meant to give you a strong warning about the deceptions and traps hidden behind the symbols, celebrations and practices that are passing as normal or innocent but actually contains a message of spiritual death. These are things that entertain you and move you away from the only truth and risking your eternity. (Jeremiah 6:16).

Preface

When I read my son Miguel Sanchez Avila's book I realized that the youth is in search of the truth about its existence and co-existence, purpose and fundament.

There is no doubt that this analysis which is most excellent to obtain for oneself and for its property; indicates a future of a better being, and when our vision is focused on the Creator of the Universe and in Him who created us with eternal purpose, is assuring our future and outcome. All growth has its crisis, the crisis of the baby when it leaves the uterus that his environment has changed from being like an ocean, to one with a unique respiratory system under development. To have an umbilical cord that draws directly from his mother to have to use a digestive system that was awarded as being unique and interdependent at the same time.

It's feeding system changes depending on its growth. All growth has its crisis when it faces change and heads towards Excellency and maturity in all what's perfect created by a Unique Creator.

If we inquire our education, doubts and criteria in our Sovereign Creator; our goals, desires and direction will be fed by the Being that designed our existed and our future will be secure. We will overcome the difficulties of our world and we will archive our purpose, to be sane individuals with a real and true vision. We will overcome growth crisis comfortably and we will each our goal, forgiving our friends that are unjust to us, we will overcome those loses of our imperfect system, our vision will not be extinguished but we will feed it with encouragement and purpose in God.

Dr. Noemí Ávila PhD, DD, DM, MDiv
President and Founder of the Ministry "Sed Llenos del Espíritu Santo"
Asevica, Inc.

Introduction

We don't have to be very analytic to determine that Christ is in our door. We are witnesses of how a loss of values is spreading in every society and culture internationally. More and more anything contrary to divine morally established are embraced and supported by the society in which we live, thus this way destroying the youth with this modern cult to Baal.

The church of the Lord is being attacked by doctrines, religions and false movements and many believe to be in the truth, but Satan is dragging them to perdition. The Bible talks in 2 Thessalonians 2:1-3, about this problem, regarding the Second Coming of the Lord: "Now we beseech you, brethren, by the coming of our Lord Jesus Christ, and by our gathering together unto him, That ye be not soon shaken in mind, or be troubled, neither by spirit, nor by word, nor by letter as from us, as that the day of Christ is at hand. Let no man deceive you by any means: for that day shall not come, except there comes a falling away first, and that man of sin be revealed, the son of perdition".

Certain Christians also enter into religiosities inside the Church of the Lord to compensate the emptiness that it's supposed to be filled already by Christ; and prefer to fool themselves living old lifestyles mixed with the Gospel. At the end, what is waiting for them is perdition. Our duty and Christians is solidify and make ourselves more firm in our faith, so that nobody can come with lies to make us fall in false doctrines that today are all over the world by the particular interests of their leaders , according to the money they can make out of it.

"And for this cause God shall send them strong delusion, that they should believe a lie: That they all might be damned who believed not the truth, but had pleasure in unrighteousness." (2 Thessalonians 2:11-12)
It is our duty to affirm ourselves more and more in God and unmask all falsehood and the entire depraved and twisted attitude that this involves, with the purpose of destroying and robbing God from His divinity.

As a young man, God has troubled me in the making of this book so that His people understand and see, especially the youth, which is more easily deceived by the commerce of modernism and its publicity through the media, without knowing the real meaning of things and what these represent.

It is my prayer that every brother that reads this book can understand fluently all the things that are here mentioned to unmask the falsehood; to get out of any deception, and at the same time, have a very intimate encounter with the Holy Spirit, our Great and Blessed Comforter.

Chapter I: The True Doctrine

The true Christian church, whether it's in the past or the present, has consisted on the acceptance of Jesus of Nazareth, the Son of God (Mathew 27:43, Luke 4:41, Romans 5:10, Romans 8:3), as Lord and personal Savior, that eliminates definitely our sins (John 3:16, 1 Timothy 1:15), whom is obeyed as Christ, the Prince of Peace and the Kingdom of God over the earth (Luke 24:36, John 14:27, John 16:33, Revelation 11:15); to whom also is given the name of "Messiah", Hebrew word that means "Anointed"; "The Prince of the Heavenly Kingdom", which corresponds also to the very meaning of "Christ", which meaning transcends from the Greek language (John 1:41, John 4:25-26)

Lord Jesus, however, prohibited his disciples to reveal this truth unto the people, until he resurrects from the dead (Mark 9:9-10, Luke 24:46). Christ promised that when he leaves, another Comforter would come to us and be with us like He was with his disciples, and would teach us what to say in the right time (Luke 12:11-12), but besides this, this Comforter will be inside us (John 14:16-17). Also, this Great Comforter would remind us all the things He (Jesus) had said (John 14:26), words that were given to Him by The Father, and which are written in the Bible, which is the Word of God, and for that reason is alive and powerful and sharper than the sharpest two-edged sword (Hebrews 4:12). The same Verb is Christ, who since the beginning was with the Father (John 1:1). Christ himself is the Word.

The church started its history as a global movement on the day of Pentecost, late spring of the year 30 AD, fifty days after the Christ's resurrection and ten days after the Lord Jesus ascended into heaven (Acts 1:9-11, Acts 2:1-13).

Christ came with the purpose of saving us of condemnation with which we dragged in the wake of the sin that was inserted by inheritance in us by Adam and Eve (Genesis 3:6). For this, He had to give his life (Romans 6:23) as a human. He was tempted in all without sin (Hebrews 4:15). Christ also suffered hunger, cold, heat, etc., just like a human; all

of this with the purpose to subject everything to himself to then later hand victory to the Church, which he also came to teach, starting with the twelve persons which He selected himself and called disciples.
The Holy Spirit, the Comforter by excellence was the one who was going to help us live life in the Holy Spirit according to how Christ himself lived and taught it; was to be God within us to overcome and carry out the Lord's work (John 16:7-11). With God in us is the only way to win, that's why Christ forbade the disciples to announce the Gospel until this promise had come to them. He specified that they would receive power when receiving the Holy Spirit (Acts 1:8).
By the Pentecost's arrival, the revival would begin. They were all waiting this promise in plea, prayer and unity. It was so big and powerful this manifestation on the 120, that they saw descend from above tongues of fire that settled over their heads. In Acts of the Apostles, in chapter 2, we can see how this event marked a triple effect:
1. The Holy Spirit clarified and lit up their minds.
2. They had a new concept of what in essence is God's kingdom: it wasn't another political empire, but a spiritual kingdom where the Lord, ascended and invisible, actively governed over their lives.
3. They received a devotion of spirit and an explanatory power such that their testimony was convincing to those who listened.
In the beginning, the theory or belief of the Church was simple and elemental. It was Paul who developed the systematic theory later on. However, there are three prominent doctrines that are highlighted in the speeches of the apostle Peter and are considered essential:

1. That Jesus is the Messiah who for so long the nation of Israel waited for, and that now ruled in the Kingdom of Heaven, whom every believer should must show three things:

a. Genuine personal loyalty
b. Reverence
c. Obedience

2. That Jesus had died and risen on the third day, and now lives as head of the Church, never to die again (Romans 10:9, 1 Peter 1:36).

3. The second coming of Jesus, in which He would return the same way he ascended, to establish His kingdom here on earth (Acts 1:11, 1 Peter 1:7, 2 Peter 3:10).

Although Christ didn't announce a specific date for His return to earth (Matthew 24:36), the expectation was he would return on that same generation.
     From this we can understand what is the fundament doctrine within the biblical context, which identifies the Church of the Lord by recognizing God Father, Jesus Christ His Son and the Holy Spirit (2 Corinthians 13:14).
It's very important for us to know how to define clearly and without confusion our double encounter with the Holy Spirit on the start of this beautiful path of salvation. This double encounter takes us to the concept of baptism. Let's see first the definition of the concept from the correct biblical perspective.

BAPTISM
It is the action of baptizing, and it's expressed in the New Testament with the Greek verb 'baptizdo', which means insert into the water, submerge, or wash with water.
The baptism in water precisely defines the death of 'self' and being born again in Jesus Christ, as Christ preached to Nicodemus (John 3:1-15). So it is understood that there are two fundamental direct encounters with the Holy Spirit in our lives as believers, which are defined and oriented to the concept of baptism and repentance in the spirit according to the Bible:

1. Transformation
Being regenerated by God, at the time of accepting Christ, the Holy Spirit begins to transform us according to the new creature born again in Jesus. At the time in which the believer accepts Christ, therefore is

accepting the transforming work of God Father, made by the Holy Spirit according to the character of Christ. In the case of water baptism, it's baptized in the name of the Father, the Son and the Holy Spirit (Matthew 28:19). The Trinity has to do with divine dealing of God with man. The unity of our triune God can never be broken, this includes all the areas, including the way God works with man. Christ himself explained that a divided kingdom cannot remain (Matthew 12:25). Our God as a Trinity is not three Gods, but one God in three persons.

The transformation will come from God because the believer wants that, and the process of sanctification will start. It's of a fundamental importance as it prepares us for our second encounter with God through His Holy Spirit and evidences us as children of God, being that this divine touch is manifested in the believer according to the fruits of the Spirit. Let us remember what Jesus said: "Ye shall know them by their fruits" (Matthew 7:16-20).

"Not by works of righteousness which we have done, but according to his mercy he saved us, by the washing of regeneration, and renewing of the Holy Ghost" (Titus 3:5)

2. Pentecost Baptism

In this baptism it is manifested in us the tongues by sign. Let us remember what Christ said:

"And these signs shall follow them that believe; in my name shall they cast out devils; they shall speak with new tongues" (Mark 16:17)

It is called Pentecost baptism because, as we saw before in the Pentecost day, in the case of the apostles, was a vivid manifestation of God through His Holy Spirit through the meanings of speaking different human languages that constitute different countries and cultures. This baptism is not just for some believers, but as we saw in the previous verse, God signalize, is a sign that follows whoever goes in the name of Jesus, awaiting the time appointed by God for a specific purpose. In the event of Pentecost, there was not one of the apostles who did not receive this baptism. Through this beautiful gift, God provides us with three advantages through His Holy Spirit to live according to godliness and spiritual victory.

a. It helps us pray as we ought.
"Likewise the Spirit also helpeth our infirmities: for we know not what we should pray for as we ought: but the Spirit itself maketh intercession for us with groanings which cannot be uttered" (Romans 8:26).

b. It guides us as to the intercession for our brothers in faith.
"And he that searcheth the hearts knoweth what is the mind of the Spirit, because he maketh intercession for the saints according to the will of God" (Romans 8:27).

c. It builds ourselves as Christians.
"He that speaketh in an unknown tongue edifieth himself" (1 Corinthians 14:4a).

This baptism in the Spirit is not part of a gift, as in the case of the gift of tongues, in which Paul speaks in 1 Corinthians 12 and 14, since in this case Paul spoke of a continuous gift in the form of aesthetic and unintelligible expression, which constitutes angelic languages.

The Pentecost baptism also serves as a sign to the unbelievers, like the gift of tongues. In order to edify believers in a particular church, there must be an interpreter of tongues (1 Corinthians 14:22).

Through the gift of tongues as a sign, the Holy Spirit also gives testimony of His work in us. The apostles testified of Christ through the Holy Spirit of God. He also gave testimony to the unbelievers of that time through the apostles (Acts 2:1-11). It was also His purpose that the apostles were completely sure that they have been baptized in the Holy Spirit, according to how Christ promised (Luke 24:49). In other historical times in which the gift of tongue was manifested as a sign, by the testimony of the Holy Spirit, was in the house of Cornelius (Acts 10:44-46), because the Jews did not believe that gentiles could be a part of the kingdom of God, and in this the Holy Spirit intervened to make

His work evident in the gentile and not only in the Jews. We can also find this in the case of the disciples of John the Baptist at Ephesus (Acts 19:1-6), whom had never even heard of the Holy Spirit, and yet the gift of tongues were given to them as a sign to confirm they had received the Holy Spirit.

It is important to know that this outpouring had been prophesied in the old testament by the prophet Joel (Joel 2:28-29) and the prophet Isaiah (Isaiah 28:10-13), additionally John the Baptist also announcement from God in the New Testament (Matthew 3:11).

Holy Spirit symbology and its meaning

We must understand that just as God the Father and God the Son, the Holy Spirit has the same attributes as God, but has a different function in us. You will know him more through your separated time for God, which should not be your spare time. Let us remember that the Holy Spirit will be the engine that drives us in the rapture to heaven to meet Christ in the clouds. The Holy Spirit has, according to the Bible, a varied symbolic representation which, in turn, describes its mission and purpose for us here on earth:

Fire

Most of the times the word 'fire' shows up in the Bible, it is figuratively as a way to describe certain aspects of God and His action on Earth. It represents his protective presence (2 Kings 6:17), His glory (Ezekiel 1:4, 13), His holiness and power (Deuteronomy 4:24), His justice (Malachi 3:2), His wrath against sin (Jeremiah 4:4) and His penetrating word (Jeremiah 5:14).

Fire burns and purifies. The Holy Spirit transforms the Christian through his sanctifying fire, burning all the dross of the old creature so that it is completely buried, and live in the Christian character of Christ, which is what gives life to the born again. Remember also that our works will be tested by fire.

As a metaphor for God's holiness, fire can purify or destroy. One example is the people of Israel, whom God purified through ordeals like Babylonian captivity. He did not want this from the start, but that happened because they did not agree to live according to God's way.

"But who may abide the day of his coming? And who shall stand when he appeareth? For he is like a refiner's fire, and like fullers' soap" (Malachi 3:2)

2. Water

Water gives life. Without water the plants, animals and humans would disappear, since its scarcity would annihilate with fervent thirst. In this same way the Holy Spirit is essential to our spirit. He is whom gives it life, that's why anyone who has not accepted Jesus Christ, lives in spiritual death (John 5:24) because the Holy Spirit is the one who can revive the human spirit and keep it alive. Note that at times in the Bible, water represents the Word of God (Amos 8:11); which as we mentioned is Jesus Christ himself, sine He is the Verb that was with the Father since the beginning (John 1:1). The same Jesus told the apostles that when the Holy Spirit arrives, he would remind us everything that He (Christ) had said. Also, Christ revealed that the Holy Spirit would teach us everything (John 14:26)

"He that believeth on me, as the scripture hath said, out of his belly shall flow rivers of living water. But this spake he of the Spirit, which they that believe on him should receive: for the Holy Ghost was not yet given; because that Jesus was not yet glorified." (John 7:38-39).

3. Wind

As the wind can clear the air and dispel the pollution that constantly occurs in the environment, so also does the Holy Spirit in the believer's life so He prevails and so the sanctification remains from its beginning through its continuous growth.

"The Spirit of God hath made me, and the breath of the Almighty hath given me life" (Job 33:4).

4. Dove

The dove, easily tamed, exemplifies the peace and reconciliation. We see the example in salvation of Noah and his family from the flood (Genesis 8:10, 11), as well in the baptism of Jesus, our Savior and reconciler by excellence.

Notice that the dove represents three important characteristics: purity, peace, and patience. Peace and patience are precisely the fruits of the Holy Spirit, which in turn produce purity because these fruits show us the character of Christ (Galatians 5:22,25).

"And John bare record, saying, I saw the Spirit descending from heaven like a dove, and it abode upon him." (John 1:32)

5. Wine

The wine makes us remember clearly that without the shedding of blood, there is no remission of sins (Hebrews 9:22). This was the price that Jesus Christ had to pay: His Blood. Also, the wine represents joy, not having anything to do with those who get drunk, as it was told to the apostles (Acts 2:1-4),but everything is represented in the symbolic spiritual typology of the Holy Spirit based on the joy we feel for our salvation.

Jesus related his teachings with the new wine that cannot poured into old bottles (Matthew 9:17), indicating that Christianity could not be able to express itself within the old molds of Judaism.

"Ho, every one that thirsteth, come ye to the waters, and he that hath no money; come ye, buy, and eat; yea, come, buy wine and milk without money and without price." (Isaiah 55:1)

6. Unity Coins

The unity coins were something that was given as a pledge or a sign of a contract, or as a security deposit of a debt. It appears three times in the New Testament, always referring to the Holy Spirit given by God to the Christians as a guarantee and anticipation of the superior blessings in the future.

"Who hath also sealed us, and given the earnest of the Spirit in our hearts." (2 Corinthians 1:22)

"Now he that hath wrought us for the selfsame thing is God, who also hath given unto us the earnest of the Spirit." (2 Corinthians 5:5)

"Which is the earnest of our inheritance until the redemption of the purchased possession, unto the praise of his glory." (Ephesians 1:14)

7. Seal

The Holy Spirit seals all those that have accepted Christ as His only Lord and Savior for the day of redemption.

"In whom ye also trusted, after that ye heard the word of truth, the gospel of your salvation: in whom also after that ye believed, ye were sealed with that Holy Spirit of promise," (Ephesians 1:13)

"And grieve not the Holy Spirit of God, whereby ye are sealed unto the day of redemption."(Ephesians 4:30)

Note also that they are seven symbols of the Holy Spirit. Theologically, seven is known as the number of fullness and perfection, which is the seven qualities of the Holy Spirit evident in the person of the only begotten Son of God, as it tells us in the following messianic prophecy:

"And the spirit of the Lord shall rest upon him, the spirit of wisdom and understanding, the spirit of counsel and might, the spirit of knowledge and of the fear of the Lord" (Isaiah 11:2)

These qualities are also evident in the believer as inheritance through Jesus Christ.

The fruit of the Holy Spirit

The fruit of which the Apostle Paul tells us in Galatians are nine manifestations in total; all founded on the principal manifestation which is love. They are part of the Christian's internal anointing. The anointing is the consecration of the believer to God, to perform divine purposes, and in this case, when we speak of an internal anointing, we know that is where it is based all of our capability to carry out our purpose chosen by God before the foundation of the world, which in turn as we had seen before, constitute our first major encounter with the Holy Spirit: OUR TRANSFORMATION.

1. Love
Agape (from the Greek word agape, 'love'), is the gift of self that makes the person who loves, as well as the desire of possessing the loved one. The agape (love) is not limited to the human field, but is also an expression of the person's relationship with God. The answer of who also feels loved is also love, which is to include all men and women regardless of race, religion or some kind of social position. Jesus is the great revelation of this form of love that should be the main characteristic that distinguishes the Christian. We can fulfill God's law through this fruit of the Spirit, which is the foundation of all others and in which we are freed from the law, because it forms in us the divine nature and buries the human nature, fallen in the Garden of Eden, and all that is divine is perfect. Jesus summarizes the law in the commandment of love to God and to the neighbor, as both are closely linked:

"Then one of them, which was a lawyer, asked him a question, tempting him, and saying, Master, which is the great commandment in the law? Jesus said unto him, Thou shalt love the Lord thy God with all thy heart, and with all thy soul, and with all thy mind. This is the first and great commandment. And the second is like unto it, Thou shalt love thy neighbour as thyself. On these two commandments hang all the law and the prophets." (Matthew 22:35-40)

The love towards God and our neighbor should always be active and definite. The idea of neighbor widens to refer to anyone who is in need (Luke 10:29-37), specifically one who is our enemy (Matthew 5:44). **"He that loveth not knoweth not God; for God is love." (1 John 4:8)**

The characteristics of love expressed in the Scriptures signify the foundation of election; as it refers to the personal, voluntary and selective. Love is in turn spontaneous, just, demands justice, is faithful to his covenant, is unique, because it demands a total response and is also redemptive. Love means live affection and is intertwined with forgiveness, which we should take as a lifestyle so we can have freedom in our heart and know that we genuinely accepted Jesus, because He is the Way, Truth and Life (John 14:6), and only the truth can set us free when we know it and accept it (John 8:32). This truth is based on love, and love is also present in forgiveness; it is the essence of Jesus Christ, manifested in us by the Holy Spirit.

On one occasion, Peter asked Jesus how many times he must forgive his brother's sin against him. Christ replied that up to seventy times seven (Matthew 18:21-22). If we multiply $70 \times 7 = 490$, we're talking about four hundred ninety times a day you have to forgive your brother. Nobody can offend another that number of times per neither day, nor anyone forgives that many offenses. What Christ meant was that if you count the times we forgive, then we are not doing it from our hearts, and the multiplication relates to forgiveness as something commonly practicable by the Christian.

In the parable of the unfaithful servant, we see another biblical example of how we are forgiven for Christ's sake the debts of others, just as God forgave us the undeserved and unpayable debt of sin, by which we were all heading for the condemnation (Luke 12:41). Otherwise, without the most powerful weapon, which is love, we cannot forgive; and God will hand us to the executioners, who are the demons, who which are planting roots of bitterness and hatred in our hearts. God cannot hear the prayer of a person without love and with lack of forgiveness (Matthew 18:15, Mark 11:25). This therefore will drive the person to spiritual failure.

When we talk about God's love, we should mention certain types that encompass this concept according to what we have defined and that corresponds to its complete definition within the biblical perspective.

A. The declared love

"**And hope maketh not ashamed; because the love of God is shed abroad in our hearts by the Holy Ghost which is given unto us." (Romans 5:5)**

B. The manifested love

"For God so loved the world that he gave his only begotten Son, that whosoever believeth in him should not perish, but have everlasting life." (John 3:16)

C. The unmerited love

"But God commendeth his love toward us, in that, while we were yet sinners, Christ died for us." (Romans 5:8)

D. The testified love

"But when the Comforter is come, whom I will send unto you from the Father, even the Spirit of truth, which proceedeth from the Father, he shall testify of me: And ye also shall bear witness, because ye have been with me from the beginning." (John 15:26-27)

"And we have seen and do testify that the Father sent the Son to be the Saviour of the world. Whosoever shall confess that Jesus is the Son of God, God dwelleth in him, and he in God." (1 John 4:14-15)

E. The corresponded love

"**The woman saith unto him, Sir, I perceive that thou art a prophet. Our fathers worshipped in this mountain; and ye say, that in Jerusalem is the place where men ought to worship." (John 4:19-20)**

2. Joy

As fruit of the Spirit, joy is not just an emotion, but a well-being and a quality of life that is based Jesus Christ and The Father's eternal and secure relationship; it is a constant joy to which we all are called to experience. Christian joy is so inclusive and permanent that it can be felt in the sacrifice for the cause of Christ; which not only means dying for his sake, as in the case of the primitive church and the many Christians today in countries that prohibit the gospel, but also includes those who scarifies their job, social position, etc., by the call as an act of faith and great devotion to our Eternal and Almighty God according to how they have been revealed the particularly divine purpose to their lives.

This joy also arises when testifying for Christ or when having a personal encounter with the Holy Spirit, whom will reveal Christ to us through His character.

JESUS CHRIST himself is the source of that joy above every negative circumstance: problems, distress, persecution, etc. A good example is Paul and Silas, who sang and sang praises to the Lord even though they had been beaten and were imprisoned in the jail of Philippi (Acts 16:25). This is proof of the joy in the midst of trouble, because it is focused on the spiritual joy, which in turn is eternal, not earthly. That joy comes because the Holy Spirit gives our spirit understanding when recognizing that we who love God and live according to His purpose or individual call, all things work together for good (Romans 8:28). Jesus himself, in His last discourse to his disciples, affirmed the promise of the realization of His joy in them, and through them to us.

"Hitherto have ye asked nothing in my name: ask, and ye shall receive, that your joy may be full." (John 16:24)

3. Peace

The peace that God promises is not a temporary peace, but a peace that surpasses all understanding and knowledge within the human reasoning (Philippians 4:7). It is the peace of the soul, is the opposite of the eagerness (Luke 8:14) which stifles and suffocates the Word of God in us to prevent it from giving its fruit. When we speak of peace we are speaking of tranquility and calmness. Precisely in the Bible is presented as part of the spiritual armor, specifically footwear (Ephesians 6:15).

The lack of peace in our lives is often due to disobedience to God; in the case of the Old Testament we see an example of the wars and the advent or peace in return for keeping God's covenant and his teachings (Leviticus 26:6). True inner peace comes from God, and is a perpetual peace emanating in us when we live in subjection to Him (Isaiah 48:18).

Precisely in the messianic prophecies, peace stands out vividly, to announce Christ as the Prince of this manifestation of the Spirit (Isaiah 9:6), and that this announced peace which will arrive through Him (Christ) would be enduring (Isaiah 9:7). Also, in Nahum, it is announced the Gospel of Peace, and Christ is the fulfillment of this prophecy. Notice that the angelic choir that the pastors in Bethlehem witnessed when Jesus was born, announced peace on earth through Christ (Luke 2:14).

"Peace I leave with you, my peace I give unto you: not as the world giveth, give I unto you. Let not your heart be troubled, neither let it be afraid." (John 14:27)

"These things I have spoken unto you, that in me ye might have peace. In the world ye shall have tribulation: but be of good cheer; I have overcome the world." (John 16:33)

Our thought should be oriented to believe in this peace, so that our mind is covered with it through the helmet of salvation (Ephesians 6:17), and likewise, everything opposite of this peace will be cast out.

"Thou wilt keep him in perfect peace, whose mind is stayed on thee: because he trusteth in thee." (Isaiah 26:3)

4. Patience (longsuffering)

In accordance to the character of many of us, patience is not easy, but we must remember that our old being has been crucified on the cross with Christ, a little more than 2,000 years ago. If we divide the word, we see that they are the union of peace and science. It involves waiting according to the grace of God to not react in an erroneous way to situations. God is patient even for those who deserve punishment for any particular sinful act, by offering a new opportunity (Romans 9:22) and time to repent (2 Peter 3:9). Christians supposed to reflect the divine patience of God in relations with others, having a heavenly firmness and not to react erroneously because this damages the gospel and our testimony as followers of Jesus Christ. Therefore in the Word, it tells us: "And doesn't sin by letting anger control you. Don't let the sun go down while you are still angry, for anger gives a foothold to the devil." (Ephesians 4:26, 27). We also need patience to wait on God's determined time', which was determined before the foundation of the world; this includes every request we make to Him, in reference to our time for a ministry calling, etc. Just as Christ subjected to the Father's patience, so that in Christ himself justice is fulfilled, so we must do. **"Who, being in the form of God, thought it not robbery to be equal with God: But made himself of no reputation, and took upon him the form of a servant, and was made in the likeness of men: And being found in fashion as a man, he humbled himself, and became obedient unto death, even the death of the cross. Wherefore God also hath highly exalted him, and given him a name which is above every name: That at the name of Jesus every knee should bow, of things in heaven, and things in earth, and things under the earth; And that every tongue should confess that Jesus Christ is Lord, to the glory of God the Father." (Philippians 2:6-11)**

5. Kindness
The kindness believer is generous and has a fervent and constant desire to do good to other people. He never accuses the faults of other, but shows sympathy to those who are burdened and helps towards the resolution of their problems. This person is pacific, gentile, very submissive and is hardly offended. This is the type of person that it's defined to us no Proverbs 15:1a: "A gentle answer deflects anger".

6. Goodness
Goodness primarily involves a meek and placid temper, and an inclination to do well. It is the product of a life filled with the light of the Lord. It's the result of a life of total consecration to God. A true believer is kind, without exception to anyone.

7. Faith

The specific synonym of faith, like the fruit of the spirit, is fidelity, which can be defined as an attribute of God manifest in the believer that's presented together with the love that saves, rescues, and forgives. God guards loyalty the same as His word given, since He honors the word that He speaks, which will not be returned back empty (Isaiah 55:11).

In Hebrew 11:1, we are told that faith is **"the substance of things hoped for, the evidence of things not seen."**, recalling further that in the New Testament does not speak about faith just as an act of attitude, always showing the concept of loyalty and obedience to God.

We can see a good example in Galatians 5:19-23 the differences between the founded works in the flesh and the fruits of the spirit, which shows that faith as the fruit of the Spirit, refers to the fidelity of the Christian. This fidelity has a driving principle: Love. In this fidelity God has reserved great reward but requires a lot of struggle, vigilance and prayer, especially in these end times (Apocalypse 13:10; 14:12)

"For therein is the righteousness of God revealed from faith to faith: as it is written, the just shall live by faith." (Romans 1:17)

8. Meekness

A tame believer is a moderate person, docile and peaceful. He has an attitude of humility, which contrasts differentiation in with what means vainglory, pride, arrogance, and insensitivity to the poor and weak person. In being tame we are in a mutual agreement with God to perform according to His direction, the humble and small works. This manifestation of the Spirit does not encourage people to defend or to respond to attackers with the same attack, leave everything in God's hands, so that the Holy Spirit personally brings a resolution to the situation or problem. The greater example of meek is in the life of our Lord Jesus Christ when he was incarnated here on earth. He also taught in the Sermon on the Mount through the beatitudes, that everyone who is meek is blessed, and was to receive for an inheritance the earth (Matthew 5:5). We can also take Moses as another example. Although the people reveled against his leadership, given to him by God, he still left everything to the Lord so He would act. His gentleness was such, that the Bible recognizes him as the most meek of all men that existed at that time (Numbers 12:3), and God always acted and protected him from any of the rebellions of the people of Israel.

"Wherefore lay apart all filthiness and superfluity of naughtiness, and receive with meekness the engrafted word, which is able to save your souls." (James 1:21)

9. Temperance

Temperance means to act with moderation, but mainly is self-control that emerges as the result of self-discipline. This fruit of the Spirit helps us to be sober (Titus 2:2).
Through temperance we'll be capable of having moderation for all things, for example: when using material goods, food consumption (Ephesians 5:8) and sexuality (1 Corinthians 7:9). Through this self-control, which in turn comes with temperance, we will be able to regulate our moral behavior through the help of God.
"For God hath not given us the spirit of fear; but of power, and of love, and of a sound mind." (2 Timothy 1:7)

The Gifts of the Holy Spirit

The expression of the gifts comes from two Greek words:

a) Charisma: which represents 'by gift', and shows that its manifestation is rooted in the grace of God.

b) Panerosis: Which goes beyond the vivid manifestation of the Holy Spirit through the members of the body of Christ, which are responsible for the spiritual growth of the church through edification and restoration (1 Corinthian 14:12)

When we speak of the gifts of the Holy Spirit, we are talking about an external anointing with which the believer, with a particle purpose from God to his person, is able to fully develop his call when it's all done according to the will of God and for His glory. When the character has been completely changed by the fruit of the Spirit, it leads to spiritual success in a mutual interaction between internal and external anointing. This function is a divine training that shows the plan of God in the person for the manifestation of the kingdom of God here on earth, and gives testimony of the greatness of our Creator.

The apostle Paul teaches that the people will have different gifts (1 Corinthians 12:29). The Bible teaches that everyone should minister according to the gift they have received as good administrators of the multiform grace of God (1 Peter 4:10).

In Romans 12:7-8, we are shown that each of us will have at least one gift of motivation as a service, teaching, encouraging, generous sharing, leadership and mercy. Unfortunately one of the serious problems today, which has caused divisions and serious problems in the church for most of its history, is that many believers have these gifts but do not consider them important. Paul gives us the example that we are all part of the Body of Christ, and each member, no matter how small he may be, is part of the body and without him it the full function of the body cannot be performed.

"But now hath God set the members every one of them in the body, as it hath pleased him. And if they were all one member, where were the body? But now are they many members, yet but one body. And the eye cannot say unto the hand, I have no need of thee: nor again the head to the feet, I have no need of you. Nay, much more those members of the body, which seem to be feebler, are necessary: And

those members of the body, which we think to be less honorable, upon these we bestow more abundant honor; and our uncomely parts have more abundant comeliness." (1 Corinthians 12:18-23)

Remember that there will come a time in that we will need to realize these things to God.

"For we must all appear before the judgment seat of Christ; that every one may receive the things done in his body, according to that he hath done, whether it be good or bad." (2 Corinthians 5:10).

All of our works will be tested like the fire; those of which that are not of God's will burn.

"Now if any man build upon this foundation gold, silver, precious stones, wood, hay, stubble; Every man's work shall be made manifest: for the day shall declare it, because it shall be revealed by fire; and the fire shall try every man's work of what sort it is." (1 Corinthians 3:12, 13).

Primarily, there are nine gifts of the Holy Spirit, which are divided into three groups:

a) *The Gifts of revelation*
* Word of science or knowledge
* Word of wisdom
* Discernment of spirits

b) *The Gifts of power*
* Faith
* Healing
* Miracles

c) *Gifts of Inspiration*
* Prophecy
* Genre of languages

* Interpretation of languages

From there on it's important that we know every gift in detail.

1. Word of science or knowledge
It's the manifestation given by the Holy Spirit to unveil a hidden truth that has elapsed in the past and reveal in the present time to deal with a determined case not known to humans.
It's a gift given only when God decides to show the person through various means such as a vision, dreams or ecstasy (Acts 9:10), audible voice (1 Samuel 9:15), speaking to the people directly to their hearts (Acts 10:19), or through an angel that God sent (Act 8:26).

The word science uses specific objectives:

a. To find things that has been lost
"And don't worry about those donkeys that were lost three days ago, for they have been found"(1 Samuel 9:20).

b. To find hidden people
"So they asked the Lord, 'Where is he?' And the Lord replied, "He is hiding among the baggage." (1 Samuel 10:22).

c. Reveal sin among the people
"Israel has sinned and broken my covenant! They have stolen some of the things that I commanded must be set apart for me. And they have not only stolen them but have lied about it and hidden the things among their own belongings" (Joshua 7:11).

d. Knowing the thoughts of man
"But Jesus didn't trust them, because he knew human nature" (John 2:24).

e. To bring knowledge of the secret plans of our enemies, tools of the devil he will try to us to attempt to destroy us. (2 Kings 6:8-12)

f. <u>To encourage the individual with discouragement</u> (1 Kings 19:4-18).

g. <u>Carry out an excellent service for the works of God,</u> in obedience to the instructions on your part, as in the case of Philip and the Ethiopian (Acts 8: 26-39)

h. <u>Supply the aid of any type of need</u> required in certain and specific moment (Matthew 17: 24-27).

2. Word of wisdom

This gift of the Holy Spirit consists of a supernatural revelation of the mind or the plan that God has about the future, which will manifest when God brings to the event and presents a piece or fragment of dreams, as in the case of Joseph (Genesis 37: 5-10), by a vision, as in the case of the apostle John when he received different views on the island of Patmos about the events of the end times; in agreement also as a symbolic representations (Revelation) through an angel also, like when Archangel Gabriel announces to Mary that she would give birth to the savior of the world, our Lord Jesus Christ, and that the Holy Spirit would form in her the humanity in which our God would embody (Luke 1:26-34), and is also given in an audible voice. An example of this case is the calling of God to Abraham, when before he went by the name of Abram (Genesis 12:2, 3).
Through the word of wisdom, the believer is alerted of any future threat that jeopardizes the plan of God and the lives of their instruments for the realization of that plan (Matthew 2:12). Also shows us the blessings to come (Genesis 28:10-15), and confirms our call to a particular ministry (Exodus 3:1-9)

3. Discernment of spirits
The word "discern" comes from the Greek "diakrisis", which means distinguish. Through discernment, God will show us certain demons that are causing some kind of divisive evil in the church, family or marriage

and that also brings disease and confusion, all to try to prevent the blessing from coming and from God's word giving fruit in its time. The Bible warns us to try the spirits whether they are of God (1 John 4:1) because not everyone who has a Bible under his arm or appears to be Christian is necessarily of God. I remember hearing a story about a church that once made an invitation to a person to preach on a Sunday. The man prayed in tongues, and before starting his message, he told to the church and the pastor from the microphone that they were not from God, and that he could prove it. He proved it by saying that he was not evangelical, but a leader of a satanic church and by praying in tongues he was cursing the church. Therefore, if the congregation had been of God as he said, they would have the discernment that he wasn't a Christian. This is a vivid and crude example of the reason behind the gift of discernment. That's why the Word of God tells us that the Holy Spirit gives testimony to our spirit that we are children of God (Romans 8:16). **"Beloved, believe not every spirit, but try the spirits whether they are of God: because many false prophets are gone out into the world. Hereby know ye the Spirit of God: Every spirit that confesseth that Jesus Christ is come in the flesh is of God: And every spirit that confesseth not that Jesus Christ is come in the flesh is not of God: and this is that spirit of antichrist, whereof ye have heard that it should come; and even now already is it in the world." (1 John 4:1-3)**

4. Gift of faith
Through the gift of faith we'll bring those things that we can't see in the physical world but we ask to God and believe with a strong conviction, to drag them from the spiritual field. This gift is given by grace when frequently having the supernatural certainty on needed miracle, recognizing that everything is done in the sovereignty of God and not of man. The gift of faith enables us, among other things, to cast out demons that cause oppression on a site, region or person as in the case of Jesus with the Gadarene demoniac (Luke 8:22-39), can also provide food in the middle of some need (John 6:1-15). It also gives us the ability

depending which is our calling, purpose and direction of God, even the ability to raise the dead (John 11:43-44).

5. Gift of healing
This gift is a vivid manifestation of the Holy Spirit who heals sick bodies, organs or limbs affected, which shows that the person who is used comes in the name of the Lord when mentioning the name of Jesus and the healing occurs. It is also testimony of the approach and the establishment of Christ's Kingdom here on Earth and in turn gives our Lord and Savior Jesus all the glory and the honor that he alone deserves. An example of the manifestation of this gift we can display it with Jesus Christ, who always healed all the sick (Matthew 8:16). In the case of the apostles, we can see for example Peter, that even with his shadow people were healed (Acts 5:15).

Remember that Jesus Christ is the same yesterday, today and forever (Hebrews 13:8). I myself have witnessed the healing of God when praying for the sick. The healing was not only for the primitive church, but also for us at the present time.

The gift of healing is manifested through prayer (James 5:15), the word that is spoken or declared (Matthew 8:8-13), laying a hand on the sick (Mark 16:18), anointing with oil (James 5:14), and also through anointed handkerchiefs or aprons that the sick touches, and in turn receives God's healing with that touch (Acts 19:12)

6. Gift of miracles
These are manifestations of healing given by the Holy Spirit in a much broader, more comprehensive and even supernatural sense. This is where cysts disappear; heals people with AIDS, cancer and diabetes; hernias disappear, the blind receive sight, the one-eyed heal, a paralytic stands, fingers are created as well as legs and arms in people who don't have them, and even raises the dead. By the gift of miracles, over thirty diseases incurable by medical science are also healed.

Besides healing in a broader sense, the gift of miracles also covers other types of supernatural events that are not just limited to heal. An example of this can be seen with the prophet Elijah. He prayed so it would not rain in Israel in consequence of idolatry, and it didn't rain for three and a half years. After that, he prayed and it rained again, after God's fire descended from the sky and burned the sacrifice, and after the prophets of Baal and Asherah were decapitated (1 Kings 17 and 18). Also as a primarily example, we can read in the Bible about Jesus's first miracle by turning water into wine (John 2:11). We can be witnesses of the story of Moses, when God parted the Red Sea (Exodus 14:21-27), and ax that floated on the water, as in the case of Elisha (2 Kings 6:1-7), just to mention some of the many miracles that appear in the Sacred Scriptures.

7. Gift of Prophecy

The gift of prophecy is an expression based and inspired by the Holy Spirit, in a language that is known by the listener, of what is in the mind of God and that He in turn wants to it to be known.

It can be manifested through praises and poetries dedicated to God (Exodus 15:1-18), the person can see written words, which in turn repeats (Obadiah 1) or can also see what God shows him about what is well hidden deep in the heart of a particular person. (John 4:17-19).

Some people may claim to have the gift of prophecy and do not, often to try and manipulate certain brothers and sisters of the church, either individually or in groups, and even the whole congregation. I want to remind you, my dear brother, that we must be alert. The Holy Spirit does not fail in giving testimony of those who are of Him.

It is important to know that the gift of prophecy will confirm in your heart what the Holy Spirit already has revealed to your spirit.

Someone may have the gift of prophecy, but it's not the same as being a prophet. The prophet's ministry is very different, since in this ministry the gifts of revelation are being manifested (word of knowledge, word of wisdom and discerning of spirits), and it's also spoken in first person (Isaiah 1:2, 7 and 14). He who has the gift of prophecy speaks in the third person (James 5:10). The prophecy is to prevent something to occur, not to try to guess someone's future.

8. Gift of tongues

As we explained previously, there is a difference to between what is talking in tongues by the gift given to us, and speaking in tongues by the Pentecost baptism.

When we speak of the gift of tongues, which is a vivid demonstration of the angelic languages that Paul mentioned (1 Corinthians 12 and 14), we are not talking about the same thing of which we are given as a sign in a conglomerate of different human languages (Mark 16:17). Precisely, the Apostle Paul's first letter to the Corinthians mentions also a difference between human and angelic tongues when comparing love as the largest and most important thing of all.

"Though I speak with the tongues of men and of angels, and have not charity, I am become as sounding brass, or a tinkling cymbal." (1 Corinthians 13:1)

Whoever in turn speaks the tongues of men and angels has both the Pentecost baptism and the gift of tongues. That's why Paul affirms and stresses that without love; even having both is of no use. Through this gift the church is edified by the prophetic word that is given in these angelic tongues when there's an interpreter.

"Wherefore tongues are for a sign, not to them that believe, but to them that believe not: but prophesying serveth not for them that believe not, but for them which believe." (1 Corinthians 14:22)

"Wherefore, brethren, covet to prophesy, and forbid not to speak with tongues. Let all things be done decently and in order." (1 Corinthians 14:39-40)

When we talk about human languages, there have also been innumerable cases and testimonies of evangelists and missionaries who have gone to try to preach to Indians tribes in the Amazon or unknown places of unknown dialect and where never anyone preached of Christ before, and when the time comes, God makes them speak in tongues, which happens to be the specific language of the tribe and nobody else knows. As in the case of which I heard some time ago, about a missionary who was preaching to some Indians in the jungle, sent by God. And when arriving, God made him speak in tongues and turned out to be the language of the tribe. Through these languages, God himself preached to them through that brother. The brother didn't know what he was saying, but at the end the whole tribe accepted Jesus Christ as their Lord and Savior. HALLELUJAH! What a triumph from God!

9. Gift of interpretation of tongues
It is a gift by means of which the person, without any mental effort, speaks what the Holy Spirit gives him to say. And in turn, not knowing the spoken language, translates everything that was said to a language understood by the believers of the particular country which they all are. This interpretation of tongues can reach our minds or our God may also be putting words in our mouth in our known language as the believer speaks the unknown language.

It is important to have interpretation of tongues in the temple, as this maintains order according to the Bible, and prevents certain things that have already happened in other churches, as in the case of the Satanists who also speak in tongues, but who curse Jesus Christ or the church and thus the congregation, which without discernment or interpretation cannot identify and prevent such an attack from the enemy.

"I would that ye all spake with tongues, but rather that ye prophesied: for greater is he that prophesieth than he that speaketh with tongues, except he interpret, that the church may receive edifying." (1 Corinthians 14:5)

The ministries

It is also important to mention that the Bible tells us about a general call to all of the believers to announce the Gospel of the Lord: "Go ye into all the world, and preach the gospel to every creature. He that believeth and is baptized shall be saved; but he that believeth not shall be damned." (Mark 16:15-16). It is necessary to remember what we explained about the motivational gifts, because through them there is also a ministry. Even the person who does the work of cleaning the church, or work as a sound, camera or lighting technician, are part of a

very important call from God and inside of any Ministry, that is their ministry.
But above all this, there are five main ministries that God raised for our edification as part of the body of Christ.
These five ministries are: Apostles, Prophets, Evangelists, Pastors and Teachers.

"And he gave some, apostles; and some, prophets; and some, evangelists; and some, pastors and teachers; for the perfecting of the saints, for the work of the ministry, for the edifying of the body of Christ." (Ephesians 4:11-12)

When we talk about these five main ministries, the anointing is different and better, and was given to each ministry in a much higher level. There is no problem for you as a believer to move in more than one ministry, but you need to ask God to reveal what is the calling to your personal life to function well and to walk into the right path. The Apostle Paul declares himself in the Bible as an Apostle, Preacher and a Teacher (2 Timothy 1:11).
God delivers a special anointing to each one of us according as He determines and to function well in His call, but if we get out of what God called us to do, we will be cause of division and stumbling in the Lord's work sometimes and we will not fulfill our purpose.

1. Apostles
The word Apostles comes from the Greek transcription "apostolos", which in turn is derived or comes from the Greek verb "apostello" which means "send" or "dispatch", and this Greek verb is distinguished by the verb "pempo" which also means "send". It involves the concept of being sent with a special purpose or official authorization.

This word appears 79 times in the New Testament, of which 68 are found in the writings of Paul and Luke and its substantive is used in three ways in the New Testament:

1. Appoints an "envoy", "messenger" or "delegate". In this sense Christ is an apostle of God.

"Wherefore, holy brethren, partakers of the heavenly calling, consider the Apostle and High Priest of our profession, Christ Jesus" (Hebrews 3:1)

2. Appoints a member of the initial group of Apostles that Christ chose, to be in a very special way his constant companions and the first ones to spread the message of God's Kingdom (Matthew 10:1-8)

3. Designates as well in the general sense, prominent teachers and missionaries, like James the Lord's brother (Galatians 1:19), Timothy and Silvanus (1 Thessalonians 1:1, 2:6), Andronicus and Junia (Romans 16:7) and Barnabas (Acts 14:14).

We can see in the Bible that the Apostles named another disciple, Matthias; to replace Judas Iscariot (Acts 1:15-26). It was in this occasion that Peter specified some requirements to be an Apostle:

1. Having been with Jesus Christ and being his partner in His Ministry.

2. Having been a witness of his resurrection (Acts 1:21-22)

Paul met the second requirement, but not the first. But claims to be an Apostle (1 Corinthians 9:1; 2 Corinthians 12:12; Galatians 1:1; 1 Timothy 2:7; 2 Timothy 1:11)

We can have the anointing of apostleship, like break new grounds and territories, build new churches, have anointing to break yokes (Isaiah 10:27), impart gifts from God (Romans 1:11), signs of wonders and miracles (2 Corinthians 12:12) and train leaders in a church (Acts 14:21-23).

The teachings of the apostles of the first century of the Christian era are the norm for life and the doctrine in the church today. This is unbreakable and can be no other "revelation" outside this

"Wherein in time past ye walked according to the course of this world, according to the prince of the power of the air, the spirit that now worketh in the children of disobedience" (Ephesians 2:20)

Jesus announced to his prophets that they would be judges in the messianic trial (Matthew 19:28) and in the book Revelation we are told that their names are engraved on the foundations of the New Jerusalem (Revelation 21:14).

It also tells us in Revelations, of those who claimed to be Apostles and were not, in one of the messages to the seven churches in the providence of Asia Minor to whom John wrote, specifically to the church of Ephesus.

"I know thy works, and thy labour, and thy patience, and how thou canst not bear them which are evil: and thou hast tried them which say they are apostles, and are not, and hast found them liars" (Revelation 2:2)

2. Prophets

The ministry of the prophet consists on the person speaking in the name of God what is reveled to him by our Creator. This includes the past, present or future. As we saw previously when differentiating between the gifts of prophesy and what a prophet is, this ministry is governed through the gifts of revelation. The prophet sees very often the spiritual field. Through the gift of discernment; he can see the danger and warn the believers.

Whoever has a prophet ministry usually operates with certain combinations of other ministries: pastorship, evangelism or in turn could also be a teacher.

According to the gifts of revelation, the prophets bring forth what God reveals to them.

"Surely the Lord God will do nothing, but he revealeth his secret unto his servants the prophets" (Amos 3:7)

They also have gray authority to destroy all satanic works and build God's Kingdom here on Earth (Jeremiah 1:10), activate the gifts in believers (Ezekiel 37:10), confirm the things of God (Acts 15:32) and also are of help to the house of God (Ezra 5:1-12). When God wants to build or erect his work, the Devil will always try to resist and cause damage to divide or destroy what God begins to form. That's why God calls the prophet, to serve him as spiritual radar to the church and thus detect any scheme or falsehood of the enemy to discard or destroy it.

3. Evangelist

Is one who announces the good news of the gospel of salvation and guides, being used and directed by God, unbelievers with qualified and anointed message, so that the unbeliever accepts Jesus Christ and begin to live life in the spirit. These new believers begin to attend church and that's were congregations also increase.

The one who has this call, God begins to open him doors to constantly be out to preach in and out of his country. He is always traveling and has a supernatural love for the souls.

God uses the evangelist with healing and miracles, since the message is addressed to unbelievers and the estranged, which need to see the power of God in action.

For this ministry to give fruit, those of us who have this calling must pray constantly so that God opens doors for us and break chains. In addition, we need prayer coverage of fellow believers in faith, every time we got to a crusade.

This ministry is very attacked by Satan because the evangelist snatches away from the devil, with the anointing of God, the souls he has captured.

"But watch thou in all things, endure afflictions, do the work of an evangelist, make full proof of thy ministry." (2 Timothy 4:5)

4. Pastors

The picture of the shepherd with his flock lends itself for the figurative use, since the Bible comes partly form a rural, pastoral and campestral culture.

As you may know, the sheep need constant vigilance and protection, should sleep in an enclosed corral, which is the sheepfold (John 10:1), and by day be led by the pastor to the field in search of food and water. Sheep are very little aggressive and need a shepherd to defend them, protect them from bad weather and heal them when they get injured or sick. Without a shepherd sheep usually die (Numbers 27:17). Jesus is the good shepherd par excellence (John 10:1-18).

The ministry of pastor ship watches over the converted souls. He disciples them, teaches them, and is always present for these people. In short, takes care of these believers, which are a type of herd. He's attentive to the members of his church, as he corrects rebel believers. God gives him anointing to restore the fallen, and ensures that no false doctrine enters to the church. The pastor also guides the people according to the correct vision of God, and constantly nourishes the congregation with spiritual food with the reason that the new creature of the person who has accepted Jesus Christ grows and yields its fruit for God.

The characteristic of a shepherd is to be always worried for his sheep, to love them and be patient with them. Today there are many who get into the pastorate but God did not call them. There are others that God did call, but have not allowed God to correct their temper and insecurity. For that reason there is so many that do not let people to grow spiritually with certain dogmas of men and that the Bible does not mention. They are just personal interpretations based on prejudice. We cannot turn up to an extremism that falls outside the divine purpose. SOME PASTORS NEED TO BE BALANCED.

5. Teachers

Teachers are those who are trained by God to lead the people to spiritual maturity through the teaching of the correct biblical doctrine.

The teacher receives passion with the fire of God into his heart. That passion will crave a constant spiritual growth of the people and also search, investigate, scrutinize and examine the Word.

Like the evangelist, the teacher also travels extensively, with the difference that the teacher teaches biblical truths to the people while the evangelist proclaims the good news, cheering and calling for the unconverted and unsteady turn to God.

The teacher teaches the divine and spiritual principles and how to apply them to everyday life.

The teacher's job is to get the text right, accurately handling and understand the word of God 2 Timothy 2:15 *"Be diligent to present yourself approved to God as a workman who does not need to be ashamed, accurately handling the word of truth"*. It means you study hard and long if that's what it takes. The teacher must be an example in life, in spiritual fervor. Luke wrote concerning that which Jesus both *practiced* and *taught* (cf. Acts 1:1; cf. 1 Tim. 4:12). No one who is careless in church attendance, who shows virtually no interest in the lost, who is addicted to harmful substances, who is known to be worldly, etc., needs to be in a teaching capacity. There are many sincere people who are struggling to overcome such problems, and for this they are to be applauded. But folks must realize that there is a certain level of maturity to be achieved before one may assume the revered role of a public teacher of the Scriptures. **A good teacher is holy**, showing "integrity, seriousness and soundness of speech that cannot be condemned." (Titus 2:7-8).

The teacher must be willing to spend considerable time in diligent study so as to be qualified as an accurate instructor of the Scriptures and must be patient and compassionate and sound in his convictions. Not everyone is gifted to teach. Those who are called and gifted to teach should do so. **A good teacher must sometimes teach hard and uncomfortable truths from Scripture** (2 Tim. 3:16) and **gives credit to God** and relies on the Father's strength. Even Jesus did this:

Jesus answered, my teaching is not my own. It comes from the one who sent me. (John 7:16).

Chapter II: Nimrod and Semiramis, the Beginnings of Idolatry.

We have devoted the first chapter to the explanation of what is the fundamental doctrine of the true church of God according to the Bible. In this chapter we will discuss the origin of paganism, images, idols, and how it has all evolved until today, showing the enemy's purpose to cover up the truth and deceive people with roads that seem right but in the end lead to perdition.

THE FLOOD AND THE ANCIENT BABYLON

We know through Genesis, the first book of the Bible, that sin entered the world by the first man and his wife, created by God, which were expelled from the Garden of Eden since God doesn't accept sin.
Due to disobeying God by drinking and eating the fruit of the tree of knowledge of good and evil, Adam and Eve were cast out of Paradise. Then they had two children: Cain and Abel. Cain, the oldest (and the first to be born on earth), was a murderer as he killed his brother Abel. Mankind was reproduced and God got fed up from the sin and disobedience of man, therefore decided to destroy the earth with a worldwide flood.
"And the Lord said, I will destroy man whom I have created from the face of the earth; both man, and beast, and the creeping thing, and the fowls of the air; for it repenteth me that I have made them. But Noah found grace in the eyes of the Lord." (Genesis 6:7-8)
Noah was a righteous man that God chose for the construction of the ark that was going to save his life from the flood that God had already determined.
This chosen man by God announced the message that a worldwide flood would destroy Earth because of sin, but nobody believed him. They just made fun of him. So, God commanded to bring into the ark a pair of animals of each species. Obviously with God's help, Noah was able to. The only ones who survived the flood were him, his wife and his three sons: Ham, Shem and Japheth, and the wives of his sons, since nobody

else believed and the rest of humanity and all living beings perished (Genesis 7:21-23).

After the flood, through the offspring of the sons of Noah, humanity began to reproduce again. Additionally to the Bible mentioning to us the names of Noah's sons, it also specifies the names of his son's children. Speaking specifically of the sons of Ham, who saw the nakedness of Noah when he was drunk, the name of these was: Cush, and Mizraim, and Phut, and Canaan, which Noah cursed (Genesis 9:25).

"And the whole earth was of one language, and of one speech. And it came to pass, as they journeyed from the east, that they found a plain in the land of Shinar; and they dwelt there. And they said one to another, Go to, let us make brick, and burn them throughly. And they had brick for stone, and slime had they for morter." (Genesis 11:1-3)

When the Bible tells us that "they said one to another", it means that they elaborated an agreement among themselves, viewed from the mundane and human perspective and not taking into account the divine one, which comes from God. These materials that are going to be used are different from those that the Lord wants; the brick is formed based on a mixture of mud, clay and straw cooked in the hot sun or in ovens. It is something that is a substitute for the stone, which represents Christ. They want to shape a religion, using a material that is not Christ, who represents the Word of God, whereby is the Verb. They prefer the waste of the fruit of wheat, the straw, which does not represent any value to God, since it has no type of conscience, and they mix it with soil which is the material of men, but not taking into account God which is the breath of life for the spirit of man.

"And they said, Go to, let us build us a city and a tower, whose top may reach unto heaven; and let us make us a name, lest we be scattered abroad upon the face of the whole earth." (Genesis 11:4)

Men do a union to build a city, which is a symbol of religion. In that city they begin to build a tower, which means wanting to reach God, but not by divine means morally established, but through the use of reason and mystical or religious experiences which are fruit of the carnal mind. They also want a name, which means a global institution respected by the political and economic powers. They also know that what they are doing is not correct to divine judgment, therefore fear being scattered since they know that the purpose of God is the union of man with Him as his Creator, not the independence of its own egocentric human prudence. We see then that God puts different languages in all who engaged in the construction, thus preventing the edification of the tower, which receives the name Babel which means "spiritual confusion to know God".

Before, there was no problem for the realization of this tower since everyone on earth spoke the same language. But after God intervenes, each one dispersed with whom spoke the same language. When scattered, they spread throughout the world creating new cities and trying to find the path that God leads them.

One of the sons of Ham and grandson of Noah, who was called Cush, whom we had already mentioned, was the main sponsor of the Tower of Babel. This man had a son named Nimrod, who also supported the construction.

"And Cush begat Nimrod: he began to be a mighty one in the earth. He was a mighty hunter before the Lord: wherefore it is said, Even as Nimrod the mighty hunter before the Lord." (Genesis 10:8-9)

Nimrod's mother was called Semiramis. Her name does not appear specifically in the Bible, but is known as the queen of heaven (Jeremiah 7:18, 44:17-19, 44:25). We also see her in the symbolic prophetic vision that the Apostle John had of a harlot drunk with the blood of the martyrs of Jesus (Revelation 17:6). There she is represented as the incarnation of a religious power that exists today but did not exist in the time of John as something "Christian." This religious power who calls himself "Christian" would bring a mix from Babylon with the Roman Empire in the future.

With this woman idolatry began to spread. Later on she married her son Nimrod, so as to base her religion and obtain power over the people. This we know through theological historical data, since it doesn't appear in the Bible. Sumerian-Chaldean was the first kingdom of the world, established by Nimrod and Semiramis.

"Babylon hath been a golden cup in the Lord's hand that made all the earth drunken: the nations have drunken of her wine; therefore the nations are mad." (Jeremiah 51:7)

"And the beginning of his kingdom was Babel, and Erech, and Accad, and Calneh, in the land of Shinar. Out of that land went forth Asshur, and builded Nineveh, and the city Rehoboth, and Calah" (Genesis 10:10-11)

Nimrod's name comes from the Hebrew translation "Gibor", which means "tyrant" or "rebel".

By For historical data Nimrod is known as a person of stout character and rebellious to God. His name "Marad" in Hebrew means "we will reveal", which indicates a "violent resistance to God".

When the Bible mentions Nimrod as a "mighty hunter before the Lord", does not mean he was according to the divine purpose. He was a big and strong man, and fierce-looking; through its ability to hunt wild beasts that constantly attacked the people, he became the hero and leader of his tribe. Like many others of his time, Nimrod knew of his Creator, but preferred to form his own laws and make his own path.

Nimrod created with his father Cush and his mother Semiramis the first great city after the flood, which became to be known as a great wonder. Later it was known as Babylon, and the name of the city Babel, also to Nineveh, which centuries later was the capital of the Assyrian empire. The name "Nineveh" derives from "Nina", name of a goddess who was later called "Ishtar". These lands are in or near to the modern Iraq. Nimrod became the richest, powerful and also most feared man of his country. He was who determined the laws, which established not to worship or even consider the God of his great-grandfather Noah. Nimrod taught his people that Satan should be venerated, worshiping objects that could be seen; like the sun, animals like the serpent and countless more things.

"And changed the glory of the incorruptible God into an image made like to corruptible man, and to birds, and four-footed beasts, and creeping things." (Romans 1:23) The name of the Babylonian god was Bel, which means lord or master. Another name was Merodach, the war god of the Babylonians (Jeremiah 50:2). In the Hebrew language the name was Baal, who was the sun god, and husband to Ashtoreth or Astarte or Ishtar, which in English is also called Easter, for which the festivities of the same name are named. It was in that ancient Babylon that idolatry was born and the root of all false religion. The sons of Cush and their father traveled to the continents of Asian and Europe, besides that they reached Egypt and Ethiopia, in the African continent, implementing the custom of worshiping the devil in the form of a snake or as the sun god. Nimrod proclaimed that Satan was a powerful being, knowledgeable of occult powers, which only he could discover. It was also there where it was created the idea of a confessional, for people to confess to the priests of Nimrod and Semiramis all their secrets and sins, since they established that they knew all God's secrets. Through this they came to gain control of everything, manipulating and dominating the people. Originally, in this ancient Babylon, the cross became an occult symbol for worship, and death by crucifixion was one of his ideas to give to those who disobeyed or broke his laws, in a sacrifice to his gods. From there came all these symbols of the hidden pagan worship.

On the other hand, by then another of the sons of Noah, Shem, whom we have already mentioned and whom had been the youngest son, had done the opposite of Nimrod. Shem on the contrary had dedicated to serve God and to be a great guide for those who wished to follow their Creator. Tradition has it that for years he opposed to the worship of idols that extended from Babylon. The priesthood of Shem was based in Jerusalem and some of the kings there were high priests called Melchizedek or Adonai-Zadek, which means "my king is justice" or "my Lord is justice". Later, according to what the Bible describes, Abraham would pay tithes to Melchizedek, as one of the high priests in Jerusalem (Gen. 14:17-20, Heb. 7:1-4).

When idolatry kept on its continuous growth, Nimrod devised by satanic revelation child sacrifice, which came to be a common religious practice, by which Shem became enraged more than ever and killed Nimrod, then he cut him into pieces and sent members of his body to the main occult leaders, the "great" masters of lies, magic and illusions of that time. Although it is also studied that Esau was the one who killed Nimrod, either way the death of Nimrod was of pain, anguish and in turn surprise for his followers. This surprise turned into confusion, since they could not explain how it was possible that the death of the sun god's high priest was allowed. That's when this system began to collapse from the ground. It was there when Semiramis, the wife/mother of Nimrod, went into action with a plan.

At the death of her son/husband, Semiramis proclaimed herself as "Rhea", which means "mother of all the gods". She also had a son which she named Tammuz, ensuring that he was born in a miraculous way and that he also was the reincarnation of Nimrod. According to historical data, Semiramis was so beautiful, that a disturbance that elapsed in Babylon ceased because they all stopped to admire and contemplate her beauty. This wicked woman led the people of ancient Babylon to worship a new image, which was of her holding Tammuz, or also Nimrod which according to her was a reincarnation.

Some associate the Genesis 3:15 prophecies with Tammuz, since it is said of him and Jesus that their births were miraculous, "lamented son", "son of suffering", but one of the two is a false messiah, since Tammuz's mother had the audacity to call herself "mother of all the gods". This prophesies of Genesis 3:15 is fulfilled with Jesus Christ.

"And I will put enmity (war) between thee and the woman, and between thy seed (which means: all the followers of Satan) and her seed (in the future, Israel/ Jesus); it (Jesus) shall bruise thy head, and thou shalt bruise his heel."

Later, Nimrod came to be known as the actual "Baal", sun god; he was also called "Kronos". To this one the Romans called him "Saturn".

If you study and compare, being Semiramis then the wife of "Baal", her title becomes "Baalti", which translated into Latin means "Mea Domina", and translated to Italian the name becomes "Madonna".

This way we can say that following the tradition of idolatry that originated in Sumerian-Chaldean, the Roman Catholic church calls Mary "Madonna", title that does not appear anywhere in the Bible.

Let me now show comparatively, the image that was worshiped of Semiramis and Tammuz (or the reincarnated Nimrod) in the ancient Babylon and the image of Virgin Mary and child Jesus of the Roman Catholic Church.

This satanic religion of ancient Babylon was able to reach more from Egypt, who then was the global power. There, the Egyptian priests believed in something to which they called "transubstantiation", a practice that they made in which they claimed to have great magical powers which allowed them to convert the sun god, whom for them was

Osiris, in a communion wafer. Is this religious rite the so called "faithful followers" nourished their souls and spirits by eating their god.
Therefore it is known that the initials *IHS* are the initials for the satanic Egyptian trinity that are: **Isis, Horus and Seb.**

The people of God (Israel) were slaves of the Egyptians (Exodus 1:8-11). They were in danger not only because the slavery and the abuse, but also because the occult satanic religious system of these people, because of this God separated them from the Egyptians and fought so they would let them go to the promised land. At that moment, God was fighting for his people against the greatest potency in the world of that time. After all of this, Egypt remained n ruins. The plagues that God sent them destroyed their crops and livestock. Also, God put grace in the eyes of the Egyptians to give the people of Israel what they asked of articles of silver, gold, and clothing (Exodus 12:35-36), and drowned the whole military cavalry when He closed the Red Sea.

As in Egypt, all the customs and pagan religions of each empire evolved: The Babylon of Nebuchadnezzar, the Medes and Persians, the Greeks and Romans. God revealed to Prophet Daniel all those empires before they rise. He prophesied before all of these empires were formed (Daniel 2:36-43).

Because of what happened in the tower of Babel, we must remember that those who carried out the construction were scattered throughout the world, once God gave them different languages. This is what explains the resemblance between the Babylonian and Egyptian pyramids with the ones form the Indians in South and Central America.

It is historically known that the tower of Babel was not of a cylindrical or quadrangular structure, but was a pyramidal construction. There we have another proof of the veracity of the Bible.

all those empires before they rise. He prophesied before all of these empires were formed (Daniel 2:36-43).

Because of what happened in the tower of Babel, we must remember that those who carried out the construction were scattered throughout the world, once God gave them different languages. This is what explains the resemblance between the Babylonian and Egyptian pyramids with the ones form the Indians in South and Central America.

It is historically known that the tower of Babel was not of a cylindrical or quadrangular structure, but was a pyramidal construction. There we have another proof of the veracity of the Bible.

I want to invite you now to take a time to look at the following table. From Nimrod, Semiramis and Tammuz was born all the mythology and diverse names taken by demons that were worshipped by empires and who are adored today, with the mask of being something "Christian", as in the case of the Catholics:

The place	The father	The mother	The child
Babel (Genesis 10 to 11)	Nimrod	Semiramis	Tammuz
Phoenicia	Nimrod	Astarte	Tammuz
Egypt	Seb, Osiris	Isis	Horus
Assyria		Ishtar	Nana, Beltis, Bacchus
Babylon		Milita	Baal, Bel
Medo-Persia	Nanacea, Anaea, Anaitas and Tanata		
Greece	Zeus	Artemis, Aphrodite, Diana	Eros
Rome	Jupiter	Venus	Cupid
India		Isis	Iswara
Asia		Cybele	Deoius

"Therefore is the name of it called Babel; because the Lord did there confound the language of all the earth: and from thence did the Lord scatter them abroad upon the face of all the earth." (Gen. 11:9).

THE ROMAN CATHOLICISM

THE CATHOLICISM STATE THAT THE CATHOLIC CHURCH WAS THE INSTITUTION ESTABLISHED BY CHRIST HERE ON EARTH AND WE, EVANGELICALS ARE "SEPARATED BROTHERS", WHICH MEANS "HERETICS", ONLY THAT POPE PIUS XII CHANGED THIS DENOMINATION WHEN HITLER LOST WORLD WAR II. IT WAS THEY WHO FUNDED THE NAZI MACHINERY THROUGH THE JESUITS (THE SECRET HISTORY OF THE JESUITS, BY EDMOND PARIS). THERE IS NO EVIDENCE THAT DURING WORLD WAR II THE POPE OPPOSED THE EXTERMINATION OF MORE THAN SIX MILLION JEWS, THERE'S NO RECORD OF EVEN A SINGLE SPEECH.

We must understand something, and is that when the Catholic Church exerts the power is like a wild lion, but when not, is shown as a meek lamb seeks unity of the "separated brothers" and all religions or try to ingratiate.

If you look in the Bible, nowhere are we told that Peter was the first Pope. In the Bible we know him as Apostle, and besides, he was married (Mark 1:30). There is a verse that is misrepresented to the extreme by the Catholics, which is the following:

"And I say also unto thee, that thou art Peter, and upon this rock I will build my church; and the gates of hell shall not prevail against it. And I will give unto thee the keys of the kingdom of heaven: and whatsoever thou shalt bind on earth shall be bound in heaven: and whatsoever thou shalt loose on earth shall be loosed in heaven." (Matthew 16:18-19).

According to Catholicism, Peter was the first Pope because Jesus made this affirmation; but according to Latin and Greek language, Simon means "sand" and Peter means "small rock" in other words, "petros", and when Christ says: "and upon this rock I will build my church", comes from the word "petra", which is "rock", so the rock is Jesus

Christ and not Peter. Those of us who have the power of binding and loosing are all who have accepted Christ. Also, the very Word says: **"Therefore whosoever heareth these sayings of mine, and doeth them, I will liken him unto a wise man, which built his house upon a rock." (Matthew 7:24)**

If we are edified over the rock that is Jesus Christ, our works for His kingdom, which will be tested with fire, will not burn; it will be like the gold.

Catholicism originated from a man named Constantine, who was a candidate to the throne of Rome, son of a roman emperor, so he felt with the maximum right to be heir. He is historically known a surprisingly wise politician and for being a great worshiper of the sun god.

On October 28, 312 A.D., Constantine fought against his main opponent: Magentius, which he defeated. Their armies faced on the Milvian Bridge, over the Tiber, sixteen kilometers from Rome. Tradition says, before going into battle, Constantine and his troops saw a symbol in the sky and in turn a sentence that said: "By this sign you will conquer". Supposedly he saw a cross, and swore that if the Christian God helped him win, he would issue an edict of tolerance so that the persecution against Jesus followers and be recognized. The only thing though, is that this cross which he described having seen was a symbol that was used since ancient times by the Egyptians, and it represented the sun god: The Ankh.

The ankh

This symbol, Constantine ordered to be printed on the shields of his troops as a signal of victory after defeating Magentius. In this same year, on 312 A.D. he took control of the government and in 313 A.D. proclaimed a decree of tolerance, giving total freedom of worship and stopping the terrible persecutions against Christians that Nero, Domitian and other roman emperors had honored by throwing the followers of Jesus to the lions in the roman coliseum, against gladiators, lighting them as a torch when crucified and many, many more cruel deaths and tortures.

Constantine also saw the possibility of roman conquest through religion. Also, he desired the support of both Christians and pagan sun and roman gods worshipers, whereby, some of the ancient pagan parties became the feasts of the church, with a simple change of name and worship.

Notice that in 325 A.D, Constantine prepared the Council of Nicea and presided as "high priest", the official title given to a Pope (Sabotage?, by Chick Publications; History Of The Christian Church, by Jessie Lyman Hurlbut).

It was around 405 A.D. that in the temples started to appear, adore and worship images of saints and martyrs. The worship of the Virgin Mary replaced the Worship of Venus and Diana, which are the representation of Semiramis. The Lord's Supper instead of being a reminder turned to be a sacrifice, like the Egyptians with transubstantiation, and the power of the preacher passed to be the priest's.

Take a moment to read something that the apostle Paul said regarding the last days and the apostasy:

"Now the Spirit speaketh expressly, that in the latter times some shall depart from the faith, giving heed to seducing spirits, and doctrines of devils; Speaking lies in hypocrisy; having their conscience seared with a hot iron; Forbidding to marry, and commanding to abstain from meats, which God hath created to be received with thanksgiving of them which believe and know the truth." (1Timothy 4:1-3)

In this verse we can see Judaism unmasked, which it prohibits consuming certain foods that were previously considered as unclean (Acts 11:1-18), but it mostly exposes Catholicism, since the forbid priests to marry. Nowhere in the Bible says that whoever serves the Lord in the ministry can't get married. Rather, most of the apostles were married. This is what we see that has attracted in many catholic priests the rape of children, married women, young girls, and even nuns. All those were and have kept being the consequences for an implantation of the Catholic Church in order to not incur expenses for the descendants of the priests.

When we talk about apostasy, its concept comes from "defection" or "revolted", which was a term referent to the political and religious infidelity of Israel, but in its prophetic or eschatological mention, as we read, refers to the catastrophic final rebellion against the authority of God, which is a sign of the apocalyptic writings of the end of the world. This rebellion is manifested to change the divine doctrine and mix it with human doctrines in order to master and manipulate to reach wealth, fame and power; like it has always been done by the Catholic Church from its headquarters in the "Vatican".

Saying that someone who wants to serve the Lord cannot marry, male or female, that indeed is a heresy.

"I say therefore to the unmarried and widows, It is good for them if they abide even as I. But if they cannot contain, let them marry: for it is better to marry than to burn." (1 Corinthians 7:8-9)

THE CHURCH OF ANTIOCH AND ALEXANDRIA

Antioch was a city who became to be the third city of all the Roman Empire, the first one was Rome and the second Alexandria; is today a city of Syria and located north of Jerusalem. It was known for its pagan worship to Daphne, which included orgies in its celebrations. Later on, received the gospel message after the death of Esteban (Acts 11:19), also where believers were first called Christians (Acts 11:20,26). It was also there where the believers started to make copies of the real manuscripts of the Sacred Scriptures' New Testament. From there, they sent missionaries to evangelize Egypt, in Alexandria. Egypt, as we already know, was Satan's territory. It was a place of occult worship, and all class of symbols that we can find today in the masonry. The people there were very proud of their great wisdom and called themselves Gnostics.

They did not believe in Jesus Christ as Son of God. Instead, the questioned the doctrine of Trinity, and also did not believe about heaven and hell. When obtaining the original manuscripts from the Christians of Antioch, they started making changes unto them.

Theologically we know that Arrius, a presbyter from Alexandria, in 318 A.D. exposed his doctrine that Jesus Christ although superior to human nature, was still inferior to God, when it's been told to us: "For there are three that bear record in heaven, the Father, the Word, and the Holy Ghost: and these three are one." (1 John 5:7).

The wiremen from Alexandria formed a school of religion and philosophy; and were used satanically to corrupt the original manuscripts of The New Testament.

Later Constantine, who secretly continued to worship the sun, ordered to a man named Eusebius, the bishop of Caesarea, to make him 50 Bibles. Eusebius chose the manuscripts of Egypt (God Wrote Only One Bible, by J. J. Ray; Which Bible? by David Otis Fuller). The Catholic Church little by little grew in power, and these "Bibles" were translated to the vulgar Latin, becoming the official Bible for the Roman Catholics.

Some of the true believers had copies of the real manuscripts from Antioch, and had to flee to the Alps and hide for their protection.

During this period it rose once again the confessionals of ancient Babylon, and the images of Mary, baby Jesus and the Apostles were added a "halo", which is the ring that can be seen on top of these "saints images", which is a symbol of the sun, and was included the "persignation", which was already used by the Scandinavian priests in the ritual of "cornucopia", which was a tradition to awaken the "third eye". Nobody doubts that Jesus Christ died in a cross, but I want to remind you that as we had mentioned, they were used originally as symbols worship and the occultism in times of Semiramis and Nimrod. Some Crosses represented the signal of the fall of the Nephilim (demons) here on Earth, the fall of the god Tyrannus, the torment of the god Wotan, is sign of the hand of the god Krishna, the route of the life and death and stringing of this world.

For the year 1950, the Catholic Church proclaimed the Virgin Mary as a goddess, because it attributed the power of being a redeemer with Christ.

Exactly how Semiramis did to add more solidity to the pagan religion of ancient Babylon. To add other more interesting notes, they also added the false dogma of "the immaculate conception" on 1854, which says that she was born without sin. The Bible without exemption says:

"There is none that understandeth, there is none that seeketh after God. They are all gone out of the way, they are together become unprofitable; there is none that doeth good, no, not one." (Romans 3:11-12)

They also added the dogma of divine assumption of Mary elevation of Mary to heaven, in 1950, comparing her to Christ, which implies that Mary never died. Where is that in the Bible?

Satan also made use of the apocryphal writing, in a series of "holy books" that was designed to try and destroy the Bible, which were approved by the Catholic Council of Trent in 1546 as divine inspiration. Precisely, from the book of Maccabeus comes the idea of purgatory. This idea contradicts everything that the Bible tells us regarding to those who die. The person who dies having accepted Christ is saved because that Blood cleans his sins, while the one who dies without accepting the Only Begotten Son of God, dies condemned (Mark 16:16).

THE JESUITS

When talking about the Catholic Church, one cannot overlook the Jesuits. If we look at history, we know that Protestantism emerged from an Augustine monk in Germany. He found in the Bible a verse that said: "The just shall live by faith." (Romans 1:17), and understood that salvation was not reached through the Catholic Church. HIs name was Martin Luther. Due to this is why Roman Catholics say that we are "separated brothers". We have to understand that God reestablished true Christianity through Martin Luther when everything was thought as lost. The world had been previously summered in the middle ages and The Inquisition, in which 68 million people including Jews, Christians, and even the same rich Catholics whom were accused as heretics so that they could keep their properties and fortunes after killing them. Luther condemned many of the things the Catholic Church did One of them were the indulgences, in which a person would pay for a document and no matter if they killed someone later or did whatever he wanted, all his sins were already forgiven. Luther established a list of 95 arguments against this falsehood.

The Catholic Church began losing power and people with the Protestantism. It was then, when Pope Paul III agreed with a Basque-Spanish man, founder of "The Society of Jesus" which is the Jesuit order. This person was born at the castle of Loyola in today's Gipuzkoa, and his real name was Íñigo López de Loyola, known as Ignatius of Loyola, who was the first superior Jesuit. They were and are today some brilliant minds whose purpose destroy Protestantism at all costs and all that according to them is "heresy", making every woman, child and man recognize the Pope as surrogate of Christ, and to submit themselves completely to his power, which is theft for the post of the Holy Spirit of God. They are currently leaded by "The Black Pope", who is in the Vatican behind scenes.

A very important fact that you should know is that on top of the catholic crucifix, reads I.N.R.I., which according to the Webster dictionary means in Latin: Iesus Nazarenus, Rex Iudaeorum, that as they establish, are the words that in the Bible tells us that were put on the cross of Christ on the crucifixion: "Jesus of Nazareth, The King of the Jews" (John 19:19). According to the extreme argument of the Jesuits it means: "Iustum, Necar, Reges, Impios; from the classic Latin that means annihilate, kings, governments, or heretic or wicked leaders ("The Double Cross", Chick Publications). The crucifix means to them an instrument of death.

Today, many churches are destroyed and divided because of the Jesuits. They make themselves look like evangelic and enter the churches to achieve the best hierarchy to then woo single or married girls and make them fall in adultery or fornication to discredit the church. There are also women who are introduced to lure the pastors and leaders to sin or spread a rumor that shatters their ministry.

One of the atrocious examples of the past regarding the intervention of the Jesuits was the massacre of the Protestants on the day of St. Bartholomew, in France on August 22nd 1575. This was where the king of France cleverly arranged the marriage of his sister with an admiral named Coligny, who was the maximum protestant leader of the country. Agreeing with the Jesuits, arranged a banquet and much celebration. After four days, the soldiers received a signal and at 12:00 midnight forced their way into the houses of the Protestants, of which they killed 10,000 people. They decapitated the admiral, they cutter his arms and genitals and dragged his body through the streets for three days until they hanged him by the heels outside of the city. HIs head they delivered to the Pope, which ordered the Catholics in celebration to give thanks to the Virgin Mary.

It's known that the soldiers were largely Jesuits and Dominican monks ("Smokescreens"", by Chick Publications). This is just to mention one of the violent and piercing events that these individuals had done against humanity. Generally those who are Jesuits are people who since children were prepared to perform, making it their devotion; there is even a Jesuit saying that goes:"Take them when children, and the possibilities are infinite".

These same persons tried to infiltrate the manuscripts of Alexandria to England, translating them to English in 1582, but the English rejected them, therefore in 1588 they tried to conquer England through the Spanish Armada Fleet. Thank God that the English weapons and the storm that broke out in the sea destroyed the fleet, if not England would be today catholic. Thanks to king James of England, who came to power in 1603, the Christian Bible was formed in the King James Version, since he gathered a group of 48 people, which God, since before the foundation of the word, had prepared to carry out this work. They were great scholars. Already in 1611 they had collected all the Holy Scriptures of the Old and New Testament.

They did not include anything from Alexandria, but the writings with which the believers of Antioch evangelized. Around 1875, the popular lament in England was "update" some of the words of the King James Bible. The ones who were behind this were the friends of the catholic cardinal Newman, whom was educated by Jesuits. Later, a secret committee was formed which worked for twenty years on The Old and New Testament. Two of those members were F.J.A. Hort (1828-1892) and B.F. Wescott (1825-1901), Romans Catholics that convinced the committee that the old texts of the Vatican (originated in Egypt) were more reliable that the texts of Antioch. Rome took approximately 250 years to damage the true version "King James". All of this has been with the purpose of definitely taking out the truth and add the mask of lies. Soon there would be a ecumenical Bible that will prepare the path of the Antichrist.

Thank God that through the puritans who came to North America, the true Gospel would later reach Puerto Rico, which is today part of the American nation, to whom we owe the evangelization in this Caribbean island, because originally it was Catholicism who arrived with the Spaniards.

Through the evangelization in Puerto Rico, were Spanish established as first language before English, God has reached to other Hispanic countries in South and Central America.

The Spaniards that arrived in the colonization also made an inquisition in these countries, just read the history and see the tortures that they made to the Indians, forcing them to worship the Virgin Mary. They wanted to take the idols from them to impose other more, covered with "Christianity". Great part of the gold they took the Vatican has it accumulated in their wealth.

Also in Europe it is known that to the "heretics", both women and men, they dislocated their arms and legs rocking them with pulleys. To the women they would cut their breasts in torture, and also tied their victims with a rope over their chest, which held a weight of several pounds, and with this torture they made their ribs break inwards, bleeding through the mouth and nose. They also burned people alive. Generally, the Dominican monks made these tortures, before the resurgence of the Gospel by Martin Luther and the Church of Rome formed the Jesuits.

The demonic principalities of nimrod, semiramis and the leviathan

"For we wrestle not against flesh and blood, but against principalities, against powers, against the rulers of the darkness of

this world, against spiritual wickedness in high places." (Ephesians 6:12)

In this verse we are warned of our fight on the spiritual field, which we can only win through the Holy Spirit, who provides us with both offensive and defensive weapons (Ephesians 6:14-18). Nimrod and Semiramis existed in ancient times as human beings, but today their names have been adopted by demons that constantly try to exert their influence over humanity.

We can show you this from the Biblical perspective with a much resembled type of Semiramis: Jezebel (1 Kings 26:31). She lured the people of God to worship Baal; killed almost all the prophets of God and practically had taken the reign of Israel, since her husband Ahab was weak of character. When God's judgment came, in the battle against the Syrians, Ahab died by an arrow that struck him between the joints of the armor (1 Kings 22:34) and the dogs licked up his blood. Jezebel was pushed through the windows by some eunuchs and fell dead, at that time Jehu, who exterminated the house of Ahab, hit her with the horse carriage and the dogs licked her flesh (2 Kings 9:30-37).

Jezebel was an idolatrous woman that also manipulated God's law, as she cunningly used the law to make Ahab stay with the vineyard of a righteous man: Naboth; accusing him of having blasphemed God and the king.

Naboth, who had refused to sell or yield his vineyard which was an inheritance of his parents, died unjustly when being stoned by the caprice of the apostate king Ahab. He paid his fidelity to God with his life. He knew that if he sold his vineyard to the king Ahab, he would use it for idolatry purposes.

What did Jezebel cared if somebody blasphemed God? What she wanted was to submerge God's people more and more in worshiping Baal (Nimrod and Tammuz), but yet she manipulated the law to her convenience. Today there are demons that ply over the name of Jezebel. There are Christians that without knowing are being seduced by this evil spirit through legalism, which is based in three objectives:

1. Manipulation

2. Intimidation
3. Domination

There's also Christians who got to the church and read the Bible and even pray in tongues, but live in adultery or fornication. These had been seduced by Jezebel. Let's see what Revelation says in the message to the Church of Thyatira:

"Notwithstanding I have a few things against thee, because thou sufferest that woman Jezebel, which calleth herself a prophetess, to teach and to seduce my servants to commit fornication, and to eat things sacrificed unto idols. And I gave her space to repent of her fornication; and she repented not." (Revelation 2:20-21)

<u>We therefore understand that Jezebel is today a demonic force that is activated thru some human actions and has taken this name to destroy God's work in the churches and ministries, the same as the names Semiramis and Nimrod.</u>

These satanic principalities always try to prevent growth in God's people at all costs, by means of religiosity and legalism, and other types of sin. That's why many churches today don't grow.

They rather seem like "denominational clubs" instead.

Through facts, we will show you how these principalities move and what is their specific purpose.

First, allow me to show you the following: according to the 12 months of the year and mentionin Nimrod, Semiramis and including Leviathan, principalities that operate every four specific months:

Semiramis (Sexuality)	Leviathan (Destruction)	Nimrod (Confusion)
This demonic authority is manifested during the months of February, March, April and May. The months in which there's an increase of incest, rapes, and where adultery and fornication is very present to an enormous scale compared to other months.	Operates between the months of June, July, August and September. That is when major atmospheric events and terrible destructions occur. It was precisely in the month of September that the twin towers in New York were destroyed by terrorist attacks in 2001.	Operates in the months of October, November, December and January. Notice the eagerness people have to buy gifts and things for Christmas. Shopping malls cannot cope. Besides that many of us christians know that the 25th of December was not the day when Christ was born. They are also months of confusion for the churches that are not well sustained in the doctrine: thus why many stray.

I want you know to see the next photo that was taken during the September 11th attacks, and that was also transmitted through television:

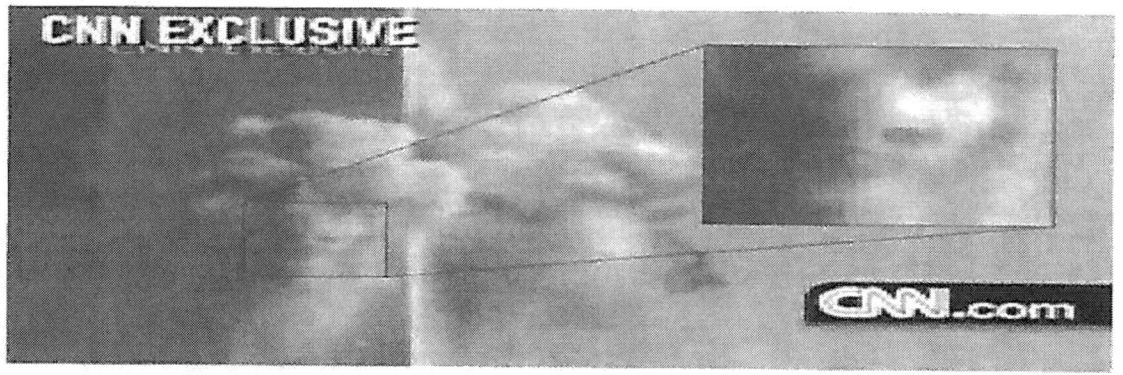

In this image we can see how it appears the face of the very Satan, with horns and everything amid the flames. People that saw the complete scene testified they had not only seen the face, but also the whole body, with tail and feet of a goat (one of the devil's symbols).

"And there shall be upon every high mountain and upon every high hill, rivers and streams of waters in the day of the great slaughter, when the towers fall." (Isaiah 30:25)

When we talk about Leviathan, in Job (the most ancient book of the Bible) its described as "a terrifying monster of the seas". Also it's mentioned five times in the Old Testament and always as an evil allied with Satan. It is also called "king of the sea" and the word connotes something basically "rolled" or "tortuous". Job also describes it as something "that estimates iron as straw" and "makes the deep sea boil like a pot", besides that it's also "king over all the children of pride" (Job 41). To which is a spirit that provokes mental blindness and three principal things: hardness of heart, stiffneckedness and stubbornness.

"His scales are his pride, shut up together as with a close seal." (Job 41:15)

Many people cannot receive liberation from this spirit because it shields between spirits of luxury, rejection, fear, shame, legalism, etc.

We cannot give liberty to pride or arrogance. "Only by pride cometh contention: but with the well advised is wisdom." (Proverbs 13:10)

Chapter III: God's People and the Idols

The diverse forms of idolatry

"And God spake all these words, saying, I am the Lord thy God, which have brought thee out of the land of Egypt, out of the house of bondage. Thou shalt have no other gods before me. Thou shalt not make unto thee any graven image, or any likeness of anything that is in heaven above, or that is in the earth beneath, or that is in the water under the earth: Thou shalt not bow down thyself to them, nor serve them: for I the Lord thy God am a jealous God, visiting the iniquity of the fathers upon the children unto the third and fourth generation of them that hate me." (Exodus 20:1-5)

The word "idolatry" is formed by two Greek vocables: "Eidolon", which sans idol, and "latria", which means worship, from there is understood that its "worship to idols". From a more profound point of view, idolatry could mean everything to which we have an excessive attachment or that we put first before God (Colossians 3:5). This type is the second form of the extreme and grave essence that represents or that comes hand by hand with idolatry, and it has always been very present inside God's people. We know that those who prostrated themselves before, and still do so today to worship images, are in a serious sin to God, but also those who have idols formed in their hearts that takes the place of Christ. Idolatry is the sin most abhorred by God, since it robs the glory that only He deserves, and it devotes it to the works that nothing are. Besides, it also ignores His eternal and unquestionable sovereignty and mocks the claims and rules established by Him in His Word. The idolater not shows significance to the divine sovereignty. Notice that the Roman Catholic Church invented thousands of virgins and patronesses in different parts of the world, and people claim and pray to them.

Precisely, sin entered the universe through one form of idolatry. We had said that there are two types of idolatry, and these can be divided in: the tangible, which is to images, and the intangible, which is based in the heart. From the intangible idolatry was the sin introduced to the universe. This was through what it is called <u>self-worship</u>, **when Lucifer (the most beautiful cherub created by God) rebelled and wanted to take the place of Jesus Christ, the Verb of God. The Bible tells us:**

"Thou hast been in Eden the garden of God; every precious stone was thy covering, the sardius, topaz, and the diamond, the beryl, the onyx, and the jasper, the sapphire, the emerald, and the carbuncle, and gold: the workmanship of thy tabrets and of thy pipes was prepared in thee in the day that thou wast created. Thou art the anointed cherub that covereth; and I have set thee so: thou wast upon the holy mountain of God; thou hast walked up and down in the midst of the stones of fire. Thou wast perfect in thy ways from the day that thou wast created, till iniquity was found in thee." (Ezekiel 28:13-15)

The self-worship is egomania, which means someone who follows their own ungoverned impulses and is possessed by delusions of personal greatness and feels a lack of appreciation.

The prophet Ezekiel and the prophet Isaiah took advantage of human types to demonstrate how the Self-worship was introduced to be the first sin of the universe, of which also surged rebellion. Ezekiel, as we read, shows us an anointed cherub. He typifies it as the king of Tyrus. The prophet Isaiah presents the Babylonian prince as a perfect type of celestial being, created by God and for His glory, but opted to take it for himself (Isaiah 14:12-19), besides wanting a glory superior to our Lord's. Many wonder how was it possible that the perfection could create so many imperfections, like it was the case of Lucifer, who today is known as Satan, which means "deceiver". We have to understand that only the perfection based on God is extremely perfect and incorruptible, impossible to adulterate.

There are many in God's people who need to be freed from self-worship. We have to remember that God by His grace and mercy was who called us to perform our ministry, but many want to exalt themselves above the Lord, both consciously and unconsciously. When Jesus gave the beatitudes, one of them was:

"Blessed are the poor in spirit: for theirs is the kingdom of heaven." (Matthew 5:3)

Poor in spirit means depending on God and give Him all of our sufficiency and act according to His will. This is why God exalts the poor in spirit; the sacrifices of God are a broken spirit, a broken and a contrite heart that we wilt not despise. (Psalms 51:17). It's an insult to God to move in our own understanding without waiting for His guidance regarding any decision. Remember that He is perfect and wants the best for us. God knows the past, present and future, and knows which decision is more convenient for you and which isn't. In our own prudence there will always be imperfection because we are human, the same will happen if we want to make a mix of the divine with the carnal to fool ourselves and so believing that we favor God and at the same time ourselves.

Do you have an idol of yourself or of something that you put before God inside your heart? Throw it out! That feeling is not of God, is of Satan.

"Thine heart was lifted up because of thy beauty, thou hast corrupted thy wisdom by reason of thy brightness: I will cast thee to the ground, I will lay thee before kings, that they may behold thee." (Ezekiel 28:17)

Love of the world

"Love not the world, neither the things that are in the world. If any man love the world, the love of the Father is not in him."(1 John 2:15)

As human beings, our existence is based on future plans and projects. There are things for which a lot of times we obsess on, our basic goal always are having the best house, the best car, and the best things which are both vital, or which are, to say, "Luxury". This world moves are based on money, for which we work in order to live. It's not bad to have goals and to want to have better things, but if we obsess too much on it and put things that we want first like a priority before God, we are creating and idol inside ourselves, and at the same time we become enemies of God. We need not be obsessed, if we look for God first, the other things that we need He is going to add (Lukas 12:31). There are people who love money more than God and only think of having more and more. The human being, in its carnal nature, only cares for himself. That's why we witness of the leaders who make decisions that affect economically that affects a particular town and doesn't care, people that also want to rise to power for their own interests of enrichment, or employers who exploit the employee and don't pay them like they deserve, earning enough money to do so. There are also people that try to wear the most expensive clothing possible, always in fashion. This shows emptiness in the spirit trying to be filled with material things, but will never be permanent, instead very temporary and ephemeral. When the person does not have communication with God, his spirit is dry and without life, since God is the only one who can fill it and bring it to life (John 3:5). The love of money and material things is what has brought misery to many countries today. People are in need while certain rulers lack nothing. The greed of the Spanish Empire by their desire of gold also brought misery and death to the colonies of America. The Lord Jesus himself said that it is easier for a camel to go through the eye of a needle than for a rich person to enter the Kingdom of God (Mark 10:25). The Bible itself confesses that the love of money is "the root of all evil", since through this idolatry and autolatry (self-worship) reaches the heart of men.

"For the love of money is the root of all evil: which while some coveted after, they have erred from the faith, and pierced themselves through with many sorrows." (1Timothy 6:10)

The Bible commands us to be good stewards and to have a balance in all things. This also includes the economic. There are many people that want God to give them what they want, but they don't ask God in prayer, nor give offerings or tithes. If we are jealous of the economic with people that we know they really worship and serve the Lord, we compare to the wicked who always spent talking that the only thing evangelicals know to do is ask for money. Such unconverted individual like these see nothing from the spiritual perspective. There are people that God calls to serve him full time, and no job is more honorable than to serve God. Then I want to ask you this question: How are churches built? From where will the pastor, evangelist, teacher or prophet eat from with his family?

Wealth and money should be used in three essential ways:

1. Tithes and offerings
Tithe is a divine commandment that is not only limited to the Mosaic Law. When we tithe and give offerings we recognize the sovereignty and control of God over our life and of everything we receive. I want to remind you, o let you know, that Abraham lived more than five hundred years before God promulgated the law and worshiped God with his tithes (Genesis 14:20). Those who say that tithes are just for the Mosaic Law has to know that there's a very basic biblical theological presupposition, starting with Abraham:
a) Abraham gave his tithes to Melchizedek, whom represented the priestly order of Christ (Psalms 110:4).
b) Biblically, Melchizedek was the representation of Jesus Christ itself (Hebrews 7:4-5).
That's why I want to remind you that there are millions of precious souls that live by tithes and offerings, that serve God with devotion, and that had left their jobs, social status, studies for God's calling. If you talk against these persons, you are against God who called unto them, and from every idle word that you speak against them you will give account on the Day of Judgment before Jesus Christ. Remember that for your words you will be judged and condemned (Matthew 12:36-37).

2. Financial management
If we are not good administrators of our finances we will not be good tithers or givers. A major problem today within certain people in the church is the excessive spending and in unnecessary expensive things, which are only bought by the caprice of showing off to others and having them. I want to let you know that this is sin before God.

3. Helping the needy

Before exercising the missionary work, Paul received as an assignment to help the needy (Acts 11:30). It is therefore necessary that we help the poor and the needy according to what God show us. There are many people today that pretend to be one of these poor people but are really not. That's why I tell you to give according to what God shows you and makes you feel. This represents a bigger blessing that to receive for anyone who actually lives in the spirit. However God will multiply everything you give a hundredfold. On one occasion, the known philosopher Francis Bacon said that "money was as a fertilizer since it only works when spread"", meaning by this that if money is not used for to promote the common good, is dung.

THE IDOL OF SEX SINS (BAAL PEOR)

Baal was the supreme god of the Canaanites, descendants of Canaan, son of Ham, whom Noah cursed (Genesis 9:25). They believed that the idols responsible for the abundance of land or of fertility. When we talk about Baal Peor, we are talking about a local version of this "divinity", since "Peor" was a Moab region. This idol was worshiped both form the Moabites and the Midianites. In these demonic ceremonies they had human sacrifices, orgies and many praises to this god. Of this idol, we cannot ignore "the doctrine of Balaam", of which there are many imprisoned believers today. The Bible talks us about this in Revelations, in the message to the church of Pergamum.

"But I have a few things against thee, because thou hast there them that hold the doctrine of Balaam, who taught Balac to cast a stumblingblock before the children of Israel, to eat things sacrificed unto idols, and to commit fornication. So hast thou also them that hold the doctrine of the Nicolaitans, which thing I hate." (Revelations 2:14-15).

We know that no curse or witchcraft work has an effect on us as Christians. In the Old Testament, when God sent the last plague to Egypt to free the people of Israel, in which all the Egyptian firstborns died, God delivered the Israelites firstborn by the blood of the lamb that they put on the two doorposts and on the lintel of each door, according the Lord's instructions given to Moses (Exodus 12:7). This typified the perfect sacrifice that Christ already made in the cross a little more than two thousand years ago. This shed Blood of Christ covers us who accepted Him, and nothing from the kingdom of darkness has power against us. Who entered the houses of the Egyptians and who God uses to hurt the firstborns, was the angel of death.

"For the Lord will pass through to smite the Egyptians; and when he seeth the blood upon the lintel, and on the two side posts, the Lord will pass over the door, and will not suffer the destroyer to come in unto your houses to smite you."(Exodus 12:23)

Satan knows that he doesn't have power against us, unless he manages to make us fall deeper and deeper in sin, which will leave us completely helpless. It will bring the same curse that God himself professed over Israel for departing and submitting to the worship of idols. When we talk about the doctrine of Balaam, in the Bible it can be read about the very know story of Balak, the Moabite king who searched for this prophet so that he would curse Israel. God prevented Balaam to do so, doing for mercy that his donkey talk, for which the Angel of the Jehovah that got in his way and that only the donkey could see, did not kill him. Important: it is theologically known that the angel of Jehovah that stops in the way is God himself: Jesus Christ. Balaam knew that he couldn't do anything against the people of Israel because of the coverage that God had over them. But in order to not lose the gifts and presents that the king of Moab had given him, he taught him the only way Israel could stop counting with divine favor: having an anathema. Balaam suggested the king of Moab to put over all the Hebrew camp shameless women with the sole purpose of leading the people of God to fornication. Of that seduction to idolatry it was needed only one step. In a very short time the Lord's people were savoring the meals that were rendered as offerings to the god Baal and prostrated themselves before him, leaving the true God to the side.

"And Israel abode in Shittim, and the people began to commit whoredom with the daughters of Moab. And they called the people

unto the sacrifices of their gods: and the people did eat, and bowed down to their gods." (Numbers 1-2)

The word "anathema" comes from a transcription of a Greek word that means "something erected" or "raised", specifically in a temple. Remember that we are a temple of the Holy Spirit, and who fornicates, against its own body he sins, which means that we get ourselves dirty as the temple of God (1 Corinthians 6:18-19), leaving the altar of God within us completely profaned. An anathema implies everything that has nothing to do with the divine, but with all the profane and contrary to what is God's, which brings damnation and condemnation. Fornication means having voluntary sexual relations with anyone who is not a legitimate spouse. The Bible is clear in that all sexual immorality is originated in the heart of men (Matthew 5:28). This also includes adultery, uncleanness, lasciviousness and orgies, of which whoever does such things will not inherit the kingdom of heaven (Galatians 5:19-21), which means that they will be eternally condemned. A divided kingdom cannot stand, it is either Christ or Satan, but God doesn't accept mixture between the two (Luke 11:14-19). Immediately when the people of Israel turned away from sin, God sent a plague that in only one day twenty four thousand Hebrews died (Numbers 25:9).

Today God is about to hurt with plague those that had brought apostasy o spiritual mixture to the church. If we have an anathema, God withdraws his protection and in His anger allows Satan to hurt us. It's a fundamental spiritual law. Balaam possessed the prophetic gift but was a materialistic person that did not care of being responsible of the damage in God's people, in order to increase his wealth and material possessions. The doctrine of Balaam consists in taking God's people to idolatry and fornication. Nowadays, Satan works even more tirelessly to bring the saints of God to impurities. Especially the youth, in a constant bombarding of pornography, either online, cable, magazines and movies. Many young people are spiritually ruined, even ministers, because of this. We must keep our eyes (Job 31:1).

Jesus Christ said that all who looks at a woman with lust had already committed adultery with her in his heart (Matthew 5:28).

Because with the eyes, we bring oppression of this sin within us and we they reach a greater degree when we commit this act that was in our hearts. There is nobody who has not committed adultery or fornication without having before thought about it.

MOLOCH: THE GOD OF NEWBORN SACRIFICES

Moloch was an idol to which was given an appearance of a hybrid being, who was half man half ox. It was entirely sculpted in bronze, and its priests stuffed him of flammable products, heated him up until it was red hot, and in its outstretched hands, which sometimes were very close to the floor, they threw the babies of the worshipers. There was also another version, in which the newborns were thrown into an oven in front of Moloch. Millions of Ammonites children died this way, since this idol belonged to these people. The name of "Moloch" in Hebrew means "king", it was also known as "Molech", "Milcom", the god of fire (for carbonizing the babies) and the god of shame for the pious men. This idols was prohibited and condemned by God (Leviticus 18:21), who had always repudiated human sacrifices. He had just ordered the rite of expiation in scarifies of Him, which consisted an animal without defect, which prefigured the sacrifice of Christ, who gave himself but to save all humanity from eternal condemnation because of sin (John 3:16). In the case of Abraham, God tested him by asking to sacrifice his son Issac, to make known to him the absolute divine sovereignty over his life, but Isaac never got to be sacrificed because God himself prevented it (Genesis 22:1-13), and in the case of Jepthah, to mention another example, we are talking about someone who didn't have a perfect knowledge of the divine ordinances, therefore sacrificed his daughter to Jehovah for an unfounded promise (Judges 11:1-39). Nowadays, people without divine fundament support abortion. It exists today so much profligacy for the woman that certain movements have come to say that "the woman is free to do whatever she wants with her body". This refers to having sex with whomever she wants and aborts as many times she wants if she is pregnant. Every woman who aborts is making a scarifies to Moloch, because they do the same thing that the ammonites did, and also does what Hebrews did, give death to a great treasure given by God, such as the children. Before the children were born, the ammonites had them already reserved for the sacrifice to Moloch, however, by abortion they actually dent even let them leave the womb. Both who performs the abortion to the woman and the woman herself are guilty of premeditated murder, since a fetus is a living being.

"For thou hast possessed my reins: thou hast covered me in my mother's womb." (Psalms 139:13)

The Moabites and ammonites were descendants of Lot (Genesis 19:37-38). Notice what it's shown of the incestuous sin with his two corrupted daughters of Sodom and Gomorrah. The sexual sins affect the future generations that are engendered in them, unless you repent and dedicate your life and your children to God.

Chapter IV: Anathema Symbols We Should Avoid

In our modern world, there is always a new fad raging from how to dress and the garments to use. These can be neckless, earrings, bracelets, etc. Advertising in the media is constant, and the secular media is not going to care if things are harmful to youth or the society in general. In order to win their audience, earn money from developers and make themselves prosperous, they can include whatever has to do with sexual or lust immorality, or all type of false religious modernism or symbols that have anything to do with all this. Of course, in the majority of the novels and movies, the evangelist (either believer or minister) is always the crazy one, and the priests the "humanity's salvation".

There are many young people who find certain symbols on clothes or jewelry drawing interesting and simply buy it because it looks "cute" or "cool", but are unaware of what these symbols represent. I have seem Christians involved in all this and do not know that it's just the beginning of spiritual coldness and attraction to the occult that the evil one will put in their lives, since they're things that belong to him. This will come to be a "hole in the spiritual armor". These anathema objects that intrude into the modern will be the main reason of our distance from God due to the door we are opening to the evil one. Many times God's people perish or die in the spiritual sense for lack of knowledge or for not being interested in knowing the meaning of things.

"My people are destroyed for lack of knowledge: because thou hast rejected knowledge, I will also reject thee, that thou shalt be no priest to me: seeing thou hast forgotten the law of thy God, I will also forget thy children." (Hosea 4:6)

Let me remind you that we are a royal holy priesthood and free from all ancestry, town, language or nation (1 Peter 2:9). It does not predominate in us the cultural nor the tangible, but the spiritual. We cannot lose our royal holy priesthood.

Next I want to show you some of the most common symbols and their meaning with the purpose of you to avoid them. I love you in the Lord and mi purpose is not to judge you, but to help you understand, comprehend and know things.

"Neither shalt thou bring an abomination into thine house, lest thou be a cursed thing like it: but thou shalt utterly detest it, and thou shalt utterly abhor it; for it is a cursed thing." (Deuteronomy 7:26)

UDJAT EYE

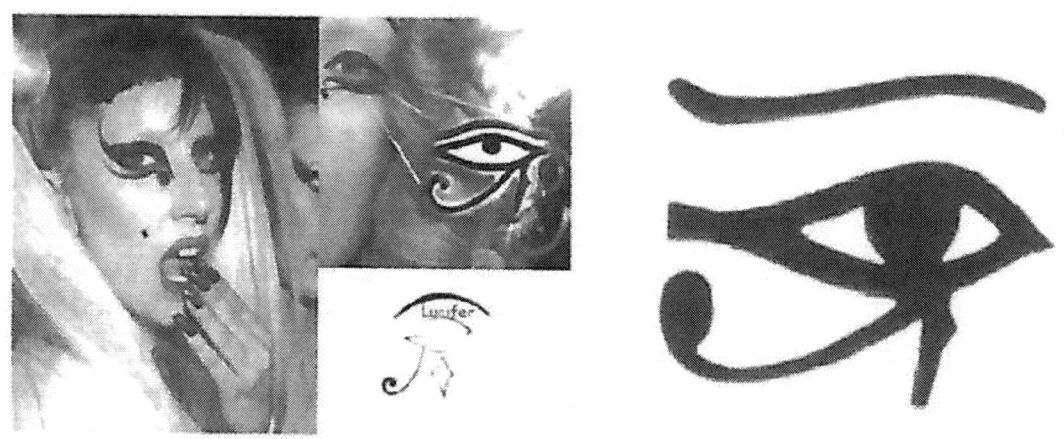

Also known as the Eye of Horus, this eye is a symbol of the god Horus as both the son of Osiris and Isis and as the sun-god. Egyptian myths state that Horus lost his left eye in his war with Seth to avenge the death of his father. The eye was also placed in the wrappings of the mummies over the incision where the embalmers removed the internal organs. Damaging the body in any way was considered bad luck for the deceased, and the Egyptians hoped to "protect it" by placing the amulet over the cut.

This symbol means "King of Hell Lucifer". The tear means the lament of all those who cannot escape his influence.

THE CATHOLIC CRUCIFIX

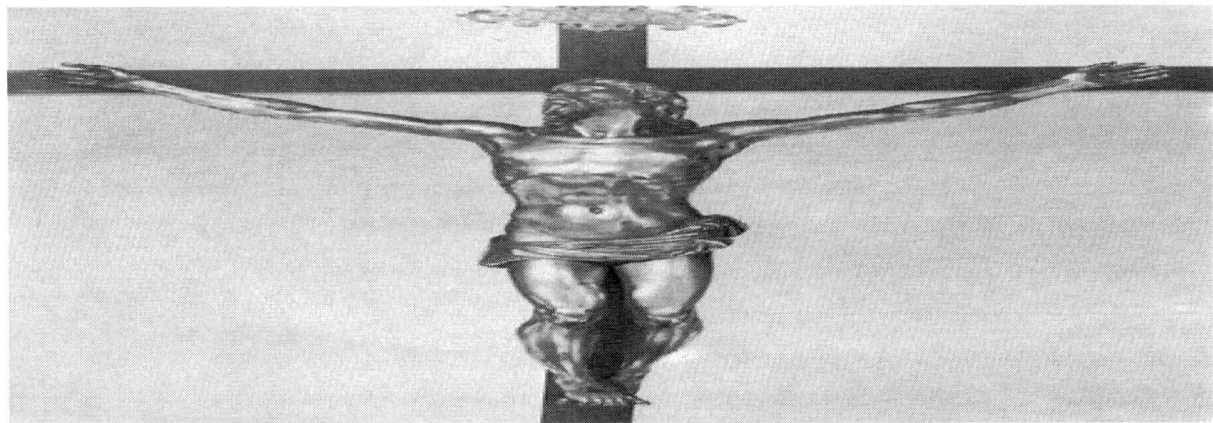

This catholic cross, Semiramis ("the queen of heavens" of ancient Babylon) dedicated it to her son Tammuz who was, according to her, Nimrod reincarnated, therefore he became the sun god, Baal. In this cross of Tammuz there is an idol of a dead "Jesus", to which the Catholics pray and worship. This crucifix itself is the center of the occult. Behind him are evil forces that emit a satanic power.

The cross has become these days in a symbol of redemption for human kind because of our Lord Jesus. He really beat the devil in his own territory, but he didn't stay dead. HE IS VEY MUCH ALIVE. He is present here, at the right of the Father and everywhere; but is good to know that Semiramis invented death by crucifixion (crucifixes were originally pagan symbols in Babylon and Egypt). You have to beware of the really meaning of the catholic institution and his symbols.

I remember some time ago, a young man became possessed by demons in the gym while he was training. His dad was in witchcraft. I saw how some people put a catholic rosary and then a catholic crucifix over him and the demon pretended he was scared but at the same time I saw how he felt some kind of power he could not resist and pushed it to the side. That power wasn't coming from God. Nothing besides that was happening again and again. The young man was not freed.

I intervened. I rebuked the demon in the name of Jesus with authority and the young man was free. After this experience I understood the purpose of the evil one's deception through the hidden power behind this crucifix. For this reason it's in some vampire movies. It has relation with the occult.

THE CATHOLIC ROSARY

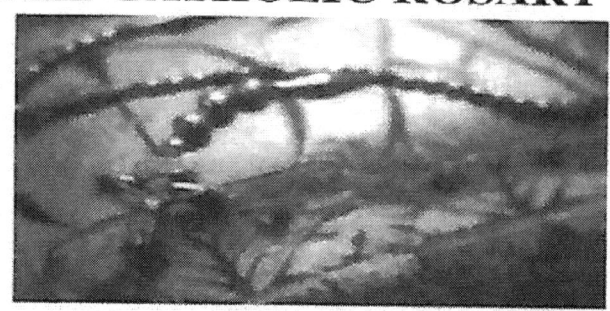

THE ROSARY IS A PRACTICE THAT HIGHLIGHTS THE ROMAN CATHOLIC CHURCH.

"BUT WHEN YE PRAY, USE NOT VAIN REPETITIONS, AS THE HEATHEN DO: FOR THEY THINK THAT THEY SHALL BE HEARD FOR THEIR MUCH SPEAKING"
(MATHEW 6:7)

IT WAS COMMON TO BURY THE PHARAOHS OF EGYPT WITH THEIR ROSARIES. PAGAN CULTS IN THE EAST, ALSO WORE ROSARIES IN THEIR PRACTICES. IN THE NEXT IMAGE YOU WILL SEE AN HINDU DEITY HOLDING A ROSARY "PAGAN WORSHIP".

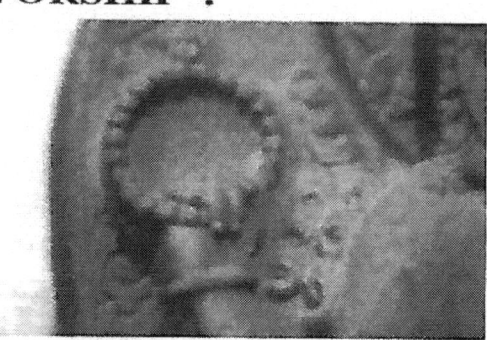 

HERE IS THE US OF THE ROSARY BY A PAGAN PRIEST IN MESOPOTAMIA

THE OBELISK

The word "obelisks", roasting pin, is a stone often monolithic, of square base, set right and ending in a point. It was put in the middle of wide spaces on the temples of the sun god Ra. They emerged from the predynastic cult to a great sacred stone that was elevated in the Temple of Heliopolis the "City of the Sun". The same as the pyramids, this monument had originally a relation with sun worship. By general rule, the obelisks erected by pairs and, according to the Egyptians, served to magically protect the temple. The obelisk consists of two parts, the body and the pyramidon and its resumed by being a pillar of four faces that look toward the four corners of the earth, being a pyramid at its upper end, which itself represents the combination of religious power and political power, for the Jesuits, freemasons and illuminated, secretly represents "a single world government". The Jesuits also had it because they waited for an American president to attest in front of the obelisk, which would be a signal that the ecumenism has finished with Protestantism, in a preparation for a concordat between North America and the Vatican.

In January 20 1981, President Reagan had sworn in from of this monument, on the west side of the capitol, where for the first time the ceremony was moved. It is not confirmed whether he knew anything about it.

Many Egyptian obelisks were taken to Rome, to the point where currently there are more erected obelisks in Rome than in all of Egypt. Before, other empires of the west also took Egyptian obelisks to erect them in their capitals cities.

The obelisk also symbolizes a sun ray, stability and creative force that had the sun god Ra. The Egyptians believed that the sun's rays to the grave had a great life-giving power that has any effect on the subsequent resurrection of the dead. It was also thought that the god existed within the structure.

"He shall break the obelisks of Heliopolis, which is in the land of Egypt, and the temples of the gods of Egypt he shall burn with fire" (Jeremiah 43:13) <u>English Standard Version</u>

By having the obelisk in the middle of the "8-step path to enlightenment" in St. Peter's Basilica, the Pope is in perfect position to "give" face the obelisk daily, many times a day as he wishes, adopting the same ritual and satanic worship to the sun god, Ra, exactly as did the Egyptians.

PYRAMIDS

They represent the trinity of the satanic idolatry: Nimrod (father), Semiramis (mother) and Tammuz (son). It is told that they emit positive electrical discharges and that they concentrate cosmic powers. They're used as instruments of luck and divination, because they supposedly contain revelations and prophesies of the world.

THE HEXAGRAM

For Jews this is a symbol of national identity not associated with the occult. This six-pointed star, if we follow the same pattern, we found that has 12 points, which are formed in the 6 triangles that compose it. This represents the twelve tribes of the Jewish people, the sons of Jacob, the Patriarch. They all contain a space, which is the way in which the Children of Israel camped in the desert. In the center was the shrine with the Levites and priests. Around the triangle, there are the twelve tribes of Israel in four groups of three.

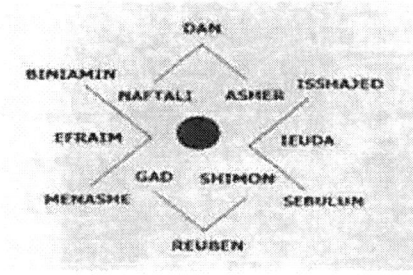

It comprises two triangles: A triangle with its apex upward, and the other with the apex downwards. This indicates the ability of human beings to climb the pyramid of life, aiming at heaven, or spiritual values. But the other down pyramid tells us that not wanting to rise and only deal with material and worldly issues, lower spiritually.

Today many are curious to know more about this Star of David, because it's also seen in the occult as a symbol. The truth is there are no reliable records that allow us to determine its origin. It is believed that it was the coat of arms of King Solomon.

Actually its origin is not clear to many. The statements of accusing the Jewish people of having a "satanic" symbol has to do many times with an anti-Semitic sentiment, and if we go deeper we can see that there is a strong opposition against Israel as a land blessed today.

Even still true that its origin is not clear, was always associated with the people of Israel, and today is a symbol of the State of Israel, the flag and the military look this emblem.

Speak about this symbol in this book has nothing to do with anti-Semitic sentiment, but to explore a little about this.

Other references states that the six-pointed star was originally a magical sense and hung on the walls to ward off evil spirits, and alchemists used it to represent the connection between heaven and earth. Some say it was in the 14th century Prague's when Jews incorporated the hexagram and in the 19th century was increasingly introduced in the synagogues and objects of worship. In 1890, the Zionist movement took the Star of David as emblem.

Others say that after World War II, Jews adopted the Hexagram not as a King David symbol, but as their representation of imprisonment and death. Israel decided to forever remember their pain and infamy made against them in the Holocaust. Today it is a crime in Germany says that the Holocaust never existed.

In 1947, driven by the Rothschild family, the Jews chose the hexagram as a national emblem of the flag. By a single vote won this design on the menorah with two olives.

Some say the true origin of the hexagram or "Seal of Solomon", comes from the religion called "Bon Po", which is the hidden and magical aspect of Buddhism. The composition of two triangles represents the duality found in Eastern philosophies. It is a symbol similar to Yin-yang which binds everything but not good and evil, because to Taoist philosophy Yin and Yang are both good and correct.

This symbol is very representative for the Masons. It's behind a dollar bill, in the middle of one of the two seals forming the word MASON at the same time.

Blue Rite of Freemasonry.

Many say that this symbol came to Israel through the wise and east travelers. Oldest hexagram in Israel is carved on the frieze of the synagogue of Capernaum and curiously beside a pentagram.

It is said that the hexagram was adopted by the pagans and occultists living in Israel in the time of King Solomon and they used it to give a graphical symbolism to the great wisdom of this king. From there, the Jewish Kabbalists discovered its great esoteric power and started using it.

It is shocking what the Bible says:

"But ye have borne the tabernacle of your Moloch and Chiun your images, the star of your god, which ye made to yourselves" (Amos 5:26)

"Yea, ye took up the tabernacle of Moloch, and the star of your god Remphan, figures which ye made to worship them: and I will carry you away beyond Babylon" (Acts 7:43)

For the occultists, this is one of the most powerful symbols used in the powers of darkness and most used for works of white and dark magic. According to the sorcerers, the key is the balance and the hexagram rules the 7 planets. It is used to awake or invoke "planetary forces".

The ankh,"handled cross" or *crux ansata.*

It represents the male triad and the female unit. It was a widely used symbol in the religious iconography of the Egyptian culture. If it is related to the gods (Duat, in In Egyptian mythology) it represents its immortality, its immanence, thus affirming its eternal condition. If it's related to men, it means instead the search for immortality, reason why it is used to describe life in contrast with death or with the idea of life after death, understood as a reincarnation. It was used to worship the sun.

THE UPSIDE DOWN CROSS

This cross symbolizes mockery and rejection to Jesus Christ. Warlocks and witches in their initiation ceremony break this cross bars made of ceramic, which means to completely turn their backs of Christ, and to sell or surrender their soul to Lucifer. The Pope Jean Paul II, on March 24, 2000, in front of nearly 100,000 people in Israel sat in a huge chair with a giant inverted cross. He also had this symbol when he was a cardinal of the Vatican.

The Catholics say that it's because it means the death of Peter, who dies crucified with his head pointing down in the year 65 AD by choice; affirming that he was unworthy to die like his Lord. Curious thing is that there are many persons who were warlocks and God rescued them and they testify having negotiated with the Pope, and that he knew perfectly who they were.

This symbol is used a lot by rockers as jewelry and frequently is shown in their album covers. The devil worshipers use it as necklaces.

THE BEETLE

For some, this symbol (also Egyptian) means reincarnation. We see it in the most of all the amulets of this culture, which for them it was of sacred origin. This beetle was very famous for the habit of rolling balls of excrement that he later deposited in its nest. The female laid her eggs over the excrement and when the creatures were born they FEED from the excrement. When the offspring ate all their food, they emerged from their nest. The amulets used to be carved in stones like Lapis Lazuli or Turquoise. The ancient Egyptians worshipped the beetle as "Khepri", which means "the one who emerges", referring to their habits, for which they associated it with the god of creation "Atum". The beetle used its antlers to roll up the excrement, because of this, it was the associated with the symbol of sun, since it was believed that "Khepri", or the beetle god, pushed the sun over the skies, the same way that the beetle pushed with its antlers the manure to its nest. If today, we see that a Satanist has it, for them it means power and a source of protection. This symbol belongs to Beelzebub, lord of the flies.

During the new empire it was used as an amulet over the heart of the mummies, which meant that the soul had passed against "the feather of truth" in the final trial. They used to write paragraphs over these amulets from the book of the dead that asked to the heart: "do not rise against me as witness", which meant the evidence that should be presented in the final judgment.

THE EYE OF HORUS

This symbol, just like the Udjat, represents "the eye of Horus", which also means "the all-seeing eye" of the franc-freemasonry. It is used for divination and psychic control, besides of all the corruption that you can imagine. It also symbolizes the eye of Lucifer or Satan, that as we know, he is the one behind all of this. Those who have it, claim for control of world finance, these are the sect "The Illuminati", which are allied with the Jesuits, to the mafia, which is the criminal branch of the Vatican; to the freemasons, the Opus Dei, the movement of the New Age, etc.

Following symbols, if we see the back of the dollar bill, we find the famous pyramid of 13 steps and, at the apex, the All-Seeing Eye symbol of Masonry referred to the Eye of Horus is an ancient Egyptian god representing the sun.

The first of Latin phrases, "Annuit Coeptis" on the back of the dollar bill, at the top of the pyramid, is translated as "Our Company is successful"

If we now look at the bottom of the pyramid, we read: "Novus Ordo Seclorum" which translated would be "New World Order". The same idea already came from ancient Babylon, building the Tower of Babel. Many say that the tower of Babel was being built as a pyramid.

Noting the base of the pyramid we find a Roman numeral, the MDCCLXXVI, which in decimal is 1776, coinciding with the year of the independence of the United States, but also the year that Adam Weishaupt founded the Order of The Illuminati.

The owl of Minerva is also a symbol of the Illuminati. This secret society was founded on May 1, 1776 in Ingolstadt, Bavaria. The goal they had was overthrowing governments and kingdoms of the world and ends all religions and beliefs to unite humanity under a "New World Order" based on an internationalist system, with a single currency and a universal religion, where according to their beliefs, each person will achieve perfection. The illuminati were abolished in Europe when its purpose was discovered, but then resurfaced another group that exists in our present.

13 is a number that is very much on the dollar bill:
13 stars above the eagle
13 floors in the pyramid
13 letters in ANNUIT COEPTIS
13 E PLURIBUS UNUM letters
13 vertical bars on the shield
13 horizontal stripes on the top of the shield
13 leaves on the olive branch
13 fruits
13 arrows

We would say that we find many times the 13 because there were 13 states that became independent from England to form what we now know as the United States, however ... for the Masons, 13, is the number of transformation.

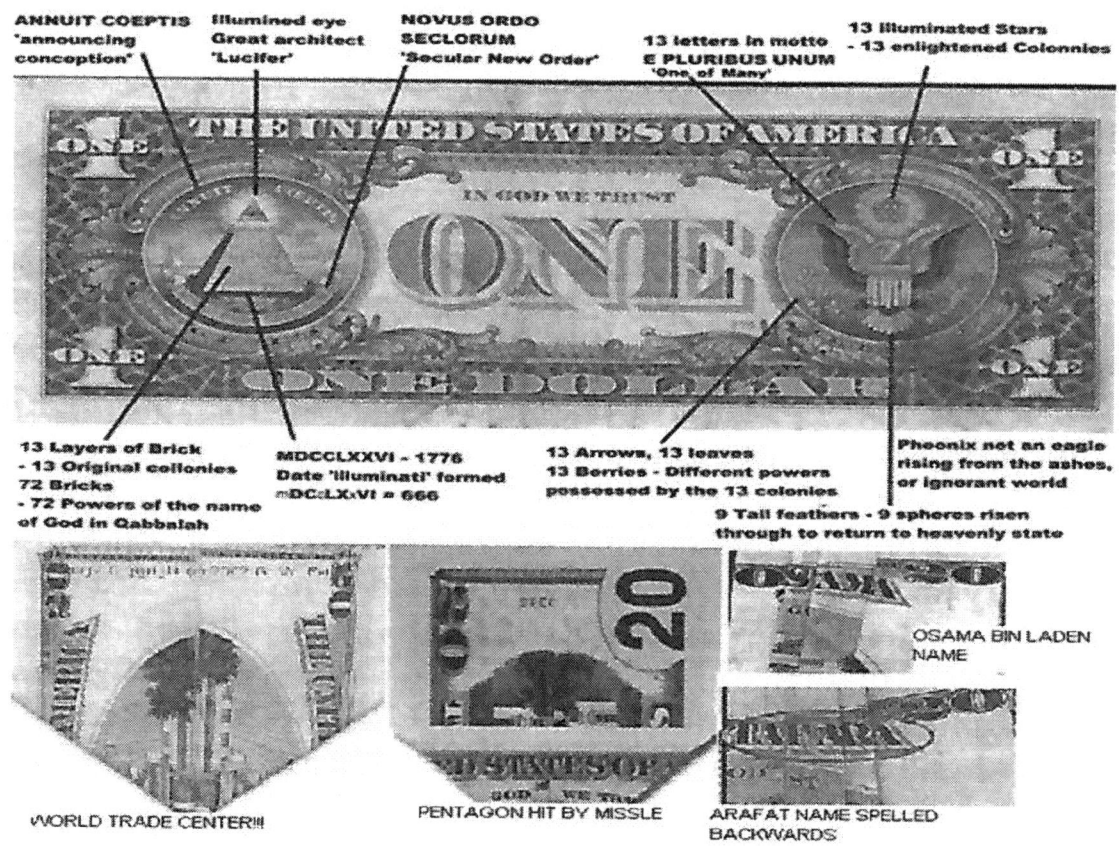

We are not trying to say to you with this "avoid the one dollar bill", but to show you how the Bible is truthful concerning their prophetic fulfillments in the next rise of a world political leader, who along with other religious leader, will rule the world in 7 years of Great Tribulation. NEVER GET THIS SYMBOL AS A SOUVENIR TO PUT IT IN YOUR HOME.

Tau Cross

It is the symbol of the god Aryan, from India, The Tau cross was also the symbol of the Roman God Mithras and the Greek God Attis. In Norse mythology, the hammer of Thor is seen as a Tau Cross. The Bull as the Astrological sign of Taurus gets its name from the Tau and Ru. Even the Druids used the Tau when venerating trees by scrawling the symbol into the bark of their sacred oaks. It's used by modern freemasons as symbol of the square T.

THE PENTAGRAM

It is used in white magic. Pythagoras, the Greek mathematician and philosopher held that the number five was the number of Man because of the five-fold division of the body, as well as the ancient Greek division of the soul. He used the Pentagram to symbolize the five Elements that made up man, Earth, Air, Fire, Water, and mind or Spirit. Those same five Elements are still represented by the Pentagram in Witchcraft today. This symbol is one of the most used in magic.

Fire symbolizes the power of desire and passion, and Earth prosperity and material goods, the air, the less personal abstractions and water, everything that is not linear or rational.

The five pointed star within the circle has been used by various people, for various reasons throughout history. It has been found in one form or another as an important symbol of almost every ancient culture. Forms of this symbol have been found in Latin America, India, China, Greece, and Egypt.

It has been found scratched on the walls of Neolithic caves, in rough diamond shapes. The Pentagram was used in Sumerian texts to mark directions, and in Babylonian drawings, where it marks the path the planet Venus makes on its travels. It was a secret Pagan symbol of the Goddess Ishtar. It was used as a symbol of all five visible planets in some cultures, or as just the planet Venus, and a general symbol for the Goddess in others.

It doesn't matter the "color" of magic, because all magic and witchcraft, white or black, comes from the evil one. Do not lie to yourself.

THE INVERTED PENTAGRAM

It symbolizes the eastern star, also known as the morning star, one of many names taken by the devil. It is used in witchcraft and occult rituals to conjure demonic spirits. It can be inside a circle or not, either way it represents Satan. Usually, all occult symbols will always be enclosed within a circle or not. When the symbol is circled, is to call a specific evil force.

IT ALSO SYMBOLIZES SUPREMACY OF NATURE ON WHAT THEY CALLED "SPIRITUAL". THIS MAY EXPLAIN "SUPREMACY" OF TWO WAYS, ACCORDING TO THEIR BELIEVES: A) THERE IS NO GOD OR SPIRITUAL PRINCIPLE IN THE UNIVERSE; EVERYTHING IS GOVERNED BY NATURAL LAWS B) COMPONENT OF HUMAN BEINGS CALLED "SPIRIT" (INTELLIGENCE, EMOTIONS, ETC.) IS A PRODUCT OF NATURAL EVOLUTION AND PHYSICAL BODY IS DEPENDING ON IT.

THE THREE PEAKS BELOW REPRESENT THE DENIAL OF THE "HOLY TRINITY" AND THE TWO TOP PEAKS REPRESENT WHAT THEY CALLED THE PARITY OR CONTRAST THAT "REALLY BALANCE" AND HEADS THE UNIVERSE LIFE, FOR EXAMPLE: CREATION / DESTRUCTION, POSITIVE / NEGATIVE, MALE / FEMALE, ACTION / REACTION, LIFE / DEATH ASSETS / LIABILITIES, ETC. Just like Taoist philosophy.

In some Wiccans traditions, the pentagram upside down is a symbol of status of "second degree" - someone who has been elevated from "initiate". For members of these traditions, the reversed pentagram is considered very positive and has no connection with Satanism, which is not true.

Some witches do their spells treading a drawing of an inverted pentagram to maintain dominated malignant energies.

Check out the next maps:

 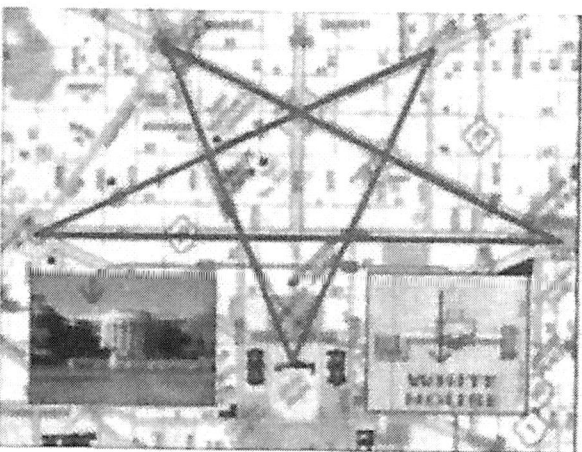

BAPHOMET

Also known as Baphometti, was a pagan fertility god associated with the creative force of reproduction. His head was represented by a ram and goat, which was a symbol of procreation and fertility, often worship in ancient cultures and ancient god of Baal cult and freemasonry.

This satanic goat inside the inverted pentagram, or "eastern star", is the "god of lust", Albert Pike, Sovereign Grand Commander of the Scottish Rite's of freemasonry, In his 1829 July 4, letter to the 23 supreme councils of the world, wrote: "That which we must say to the crowd is we worship a god but it is the god that one adores without superstition.",, "you may repeat it to the 32nd, 31st and 30th degrees the Masonic religion should be by all of us initiates of the high degrees maintained in the purity of the Lucifarian doctrine. ... The true and pure philosophic religion is the belief in Lucifer the equal of Adonay [Jesus]."

Lucifer, According to Pike is God. BLASPHEMY!

Albert Pike's Book Morals and Dogma:

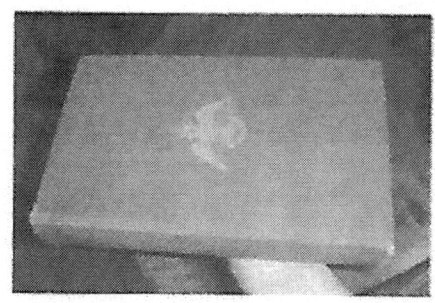

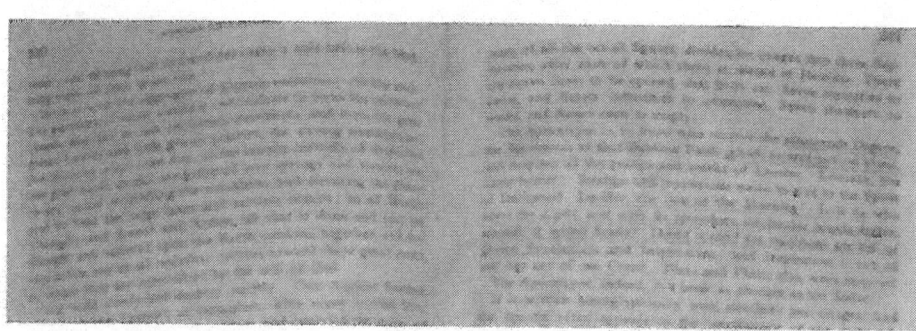

This symbol identifies almost all Masonic lodges. It consists of a compass, a square and a letter G in the center, which actually means the male sexual organ, the representation of Venus (another name for Lucifer) and the word gnosis, generation and large.

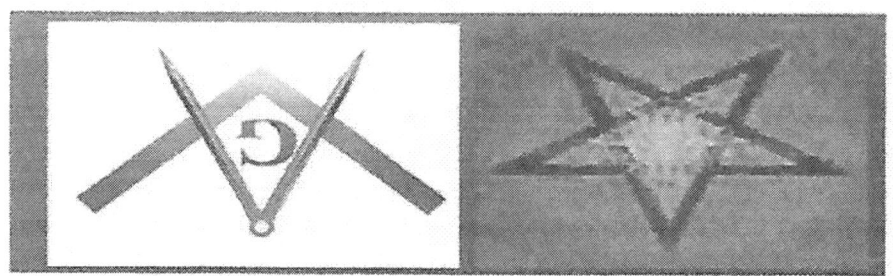

Swastika or sun wheel

It was used way before the Nazis and their leader, Hitler. It was used on Greek coins, Buddhist inscriptions and Celtic monuments. It had its start in ancient Babylon, and means the course of the sun in the skies. Represents the power of the boomerang, in which, everything that goes up has to come down, and everything you do is returned to you.

Hitler was into the occult beliefs and became known as a Roman Catholic. He adopted this symbol to represent the Nazi party.

In the next picture you can see the swastika in different cultures and charms:

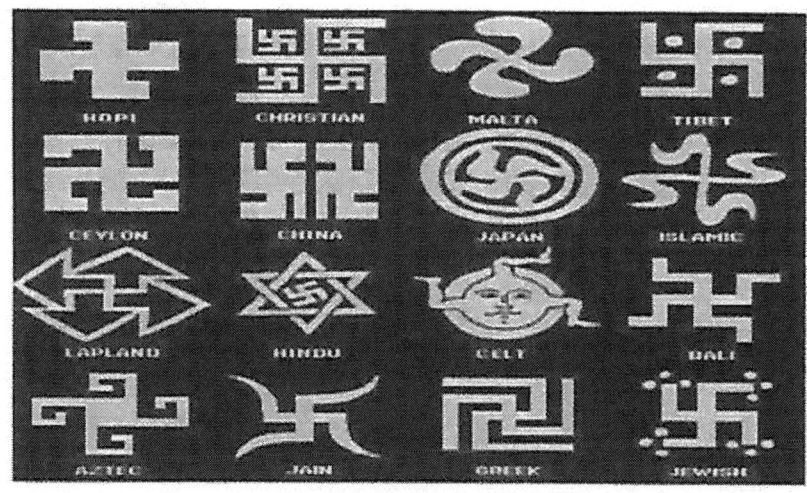

THE ITALIAN HORN

Some say that it has to do with the horse with wings and a horn on its forehead, which is the mythological unicorn. It was introduced by the druids of Scotland and Ireland. It's associated with the good luck and the good fortune. It is also used as the "evil eye". Also, it means that Satan will take control of your finances.

Before the advent of Catholicism in Italy, the Moon goddess was considered very sacred. She had horns. Thus, horn shaped jewelry was worn to show respect for the moon goddess as well as to ward off any evil, according to their superstition. When Catholicism took roots in Italy, the moon goddess was replaced by the Virgin Mary, who was shown to be standing on a lunar crescent. Thus, horns remained sacred for all. Other beliefs indicate the horns as having sexual powers and bestowing good luck on the wearer. Sometimes the horn is worn along with a cross for better protection against all kinds of evils.

We don't need this to protection. We have the Jesus Almighty blood that protects us when we believe in Him. The Devil use all kind of superstitions to chain those who believe in this. He will make difficult to open the spiritual jail for his prisoners, but with the power of Jesus, EVERYTHING is possible.

The Ouroboros

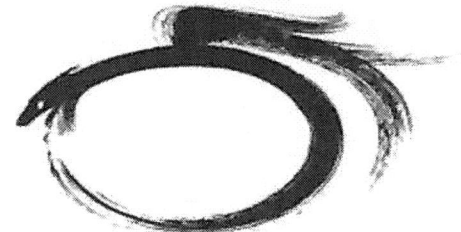

The Ouroboros is an ancient symbol depicting a serpent or dragon eating its own tail. The name originates from within Greek language; (oura) meaning "tail" and (boros) meaning "eating", thus "he who eats the tail". The Ouroboros represents the perpetual cyclic renewal of life and infinity, the concept of eternity and the eternal return, and represents the cycle of life, death and rebirth, leading to immortality, as in the Phoenix, the mythical sacred firebird that can be found in the mythologies of the Egyptians, Arabian, Persians, Greeks, Romans, Chinese, Hindu, Phoenicians, Mesoamericans, Native Americans, and more.

This also represents the dragon, symbolizing "the alpha and omega", attribute that really belongs to Jesus Christ who is the Beginning and the End. These are the first and last letters of the Greek alphabet. The circle is a symbol of the sun god and Lucifer. Like we mention before, occultists use it to summon demonic powers. An example of this we can see in the old movie "The Ring" (2002). Beware of what kind of movie you take home to watch. There are many new movies in this times coming out with so much occult content and they are open doors to the enemy. Christians will dedicate all to God. Who do you think the occultists devoted what they do?

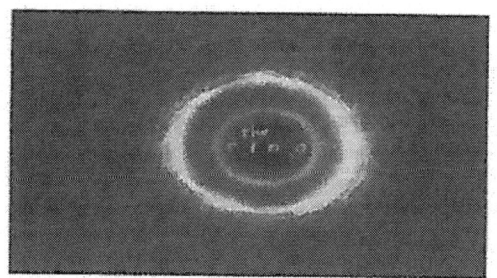 

ANARCHY

It means to abolish all laws. In other words, "do whatever you want". This is the law of the Satanists. This symbol is used by the "punks", rockers and followers of heavy metal.

It is sad to say that this is popular among school aged children today; this symbol for anarchy fits the message that pervades the most popular video games, role-playing games, movies and television. The lines of the "A" often extend outside the circle.

To many Satanists and other fast-growing occult groups it represents their slogan, "do what thou wilt." Some former occultists have explained that it represents the **ASMODEAS:** a demonic force driving teenagers toward sexual perversion and suicide.

Broken Cross
Also called a Neronic Cross or a Stipe

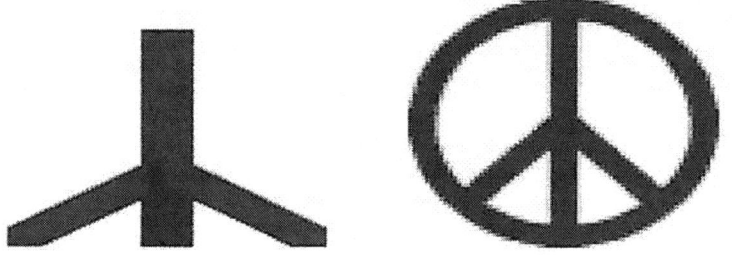

It is also known as a sign of "love and peace", used by the hippies. Another symbol that mocks the sacrifice of Jesus on the cross. It also means: the ruins of the dead man. It appeared in some of the canes of the SS of Hitler.

Enclosed in a circle, the Broken Cross has been the emblem of the Campaign for Nuclear Disarmament since 1958 and the symbol has become synonymous with 'Peace'.

Satanists used this symbol in the middle Ages as a mockery of Christianity. A broken cross or inverted cross means to say that Christ stayed dead and the denial to him as God. It represents that Christ was defeated at the cross of Calvary.

There is also the theory that this symbol has been introduced by the Illuminati as part of the global conspiracy in the 60s by a completely opposite meaning to real to make everyone use this sign without actually knowing its true history.

Super Computer "The Beast".
Brussels, Belgium.

The yin-yang

 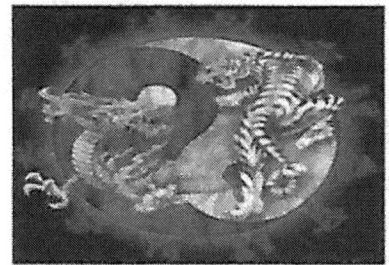

The image consists of a circle divided into two teardrop-shaped halves - one white and the other black. Within each half is contained a smaller circle of the opposite color. We have already explained the likeness between occultist's symbols and Taoist philosophy. I think now it will be easier for you to understand why as Christians we should not have this symbol.

Many misunderstand that sometimes when we are talking about this symbol; we are trying to ban karate. But one thing is exercise, which is not bad, and otherwise are Eastern philosophies. Additionally, this symbol is CHINESE origin therefore has NOTHING TO DO WITH THE KARATE BUT WITH KUNG FU AND TAI CHI. KARATE IS FROM JAPAN.

The yin-yang is a concept born of Eastern philosophy based on the duality of everything in the universe. It describes the two opposing but complementary fundamental forces found in all things. According to this view every being, object or thought has a complement that depends for its existence and that in turn exists within them, deducting from this that nothing exists in a pure state, either in absolute stillness, but a continuous transformation.

THE SATANIC CROSS

This cross has a question mark below it, which means questioning God's deity, and inside the occultism it represents the three crowned princes: Satan (also Lucifer), Belial and Leviathan. It also means subjection to the domain of Lucifer.

THE STAR AND CRESCENT

Represents the goddess of the moon Diana, or Diana of the Ephesians (Acts 19:23-41) and the "morning star", Lucifer's name (Isaiah 14:12). Witchcraft uses this symbol to show the way to Satanism and Satanism uses it in the opposite direction to show the way to witchcraft. The crescent moon is seen everywhere in the Islamic world. On 1950, some archaeologists found an idol of the name Allah, sitting with the crescent moon on its chest, in excavations at Hazor, Palestine. It turns out that "Allah" was the name of one of the idols of the Quraysh tribe of Muhammad.

HORNED HAND

This is the sign of recognition between those who are involved in the occult. Notice the thumb over the fingers and it's done with the left hand most of the time. It means literally, the holy trinity of God rendered to the horns of Satan. This is a very big blasphemy.

There is a difference between the horned hands and the meaning of "I love you", in the deaf- mute language. IT'S NOT THE SAME.

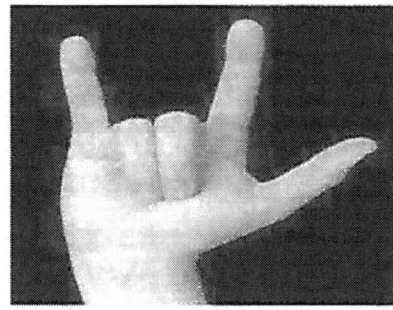
"I love you", in the deaf- mute language

Horned hand

The horned hand is very common among singers of Rock, pop and heavy metal, but has also been used by actors and prominent public and political figures these days.

CRESCENT SIGN

It was used to greet the crescent. Today the surfers and the soccer players use it like something cool. It's said to be the secret handshake between Satanists and witches.

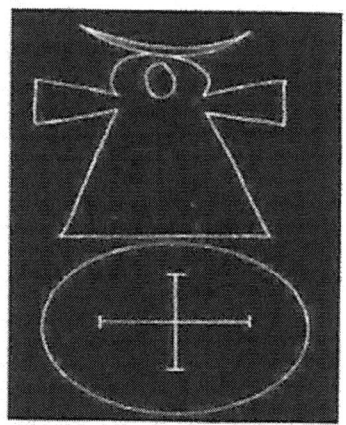

This satanic symbol is used to indicate that a black mass has taken place or will take place where this symbol is. Can you see the crescent?

Blood ritual

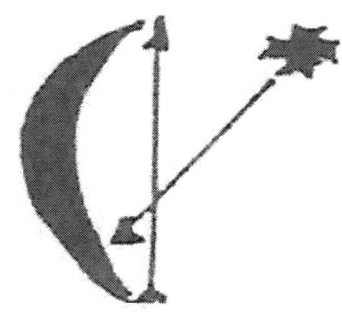

This symbol represents the ritual slaughter of animals and humans, and naturally is associated with the Devil. Those sacrifices are in Black Magic. There, you see the crescent again.

Sexual ritual

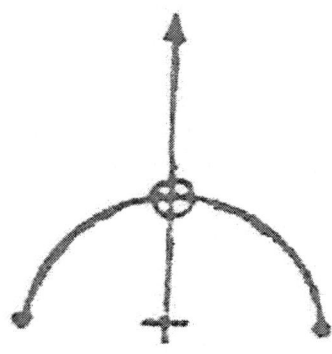

This symbol, typical of black magic, represents that it has made or will be make a sexual ritual. Crescent backwards.

THE SKULL

It is the symbol of death and used to curse. In satanic rituals it serves as recipient to place the blood of the sacrifices. On occasions it is used by young people on necklaces, rings and different jewelry. The negative influence is very strong when used. Be very careful.

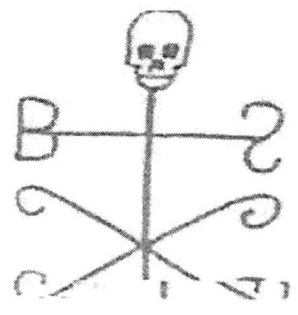

These symbols are used in voodoo, and voodoo is actually a form very close to practice Satanism as it is usually expressed as black magic.

In the next picture you will see a voodoo priestess kissing the ground. For them, "The earth is not only kissing before men and gods, also in front of the holy objects"

Priestess pronounces the names of deities and bows three times to the ground and kisses. Just like Pope John Paul II used to do.

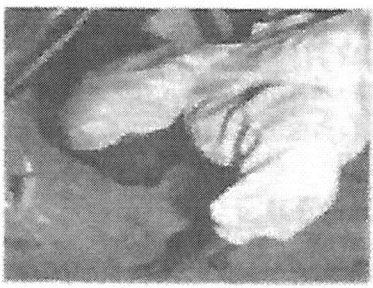 

Pope Juan Paul II with voodoo Priests

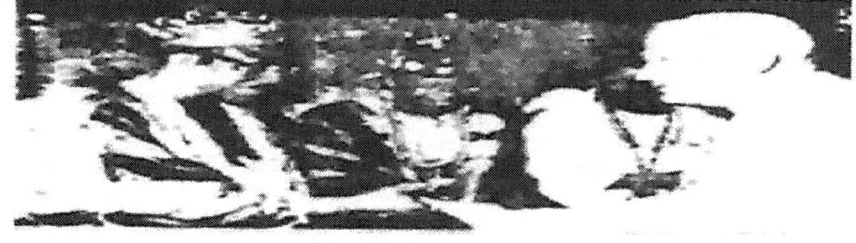

THE SATANIC "S"

It represents a "lightning bolt", which means "destructor". On mythology, it was Zeus' weapon. Worn on the body or on clothes means power over others. Also, it was used by the feared "SS" of the Nazi Germany (SS= serving Satan?). I invite you now to read this biblical text: "How art thou fallen from heaven, O Lucifer, son of the morning! How art thou cut down to the ground, which didst weaken the nations?" (Isaiah 14:12). Remember the fall of Satan?

NAZI UNIFORM   **NAZI RING**   **POKEMON**

In the Nazi uniform you can also find a **PATE CROSS,** also used in the Papal Pallium.

I want you now to see the next image of Shamshi-**Adad V**, who was the **king** of Assyria from 824 to 811 BC. This cross symbolized the pagan worship of the sun god. This same cross is on the chest of this king.

 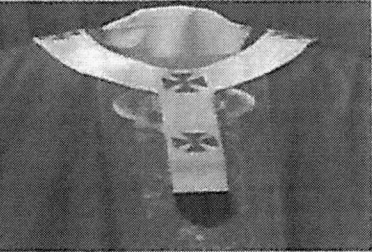 

TRIQUETRA

    This is an ancient symbol of over 5500 years old which could cover much of Europe, including the Nordic countries and the British Isles. Its origin is Celtic and symbolizes death and rebirth and the three forces of the universe: earth, water and fire, represents the triple goddess (maiden, mother and crone), equality, eternity and invisibility. This symbol, as a talisman, is considered to represent the mind, body and soul and the domains of land, sea and sky.

    Triquetras are composed of a combination of three circles in different ways to describe the worship of three much worshiped pagan deities through the centuries:

    1. Isis (Semiramis, Ishtar, Aphrodite, Venus, Astarte, Cybele, Mary).

    2. Osiris (Nimrod).

    3. Horus (Tammuz, Baal, Bel, Belial, Cupid, Eros, Satan, Saturn, Kronos, Sun Set)

    THIS SYMBOL HAS NOTHING TO DO WITH CHRISTIANITY OR THE HOLY TRINITY. The intent is to introduce new era in churches. The Triquetras can also be enclosed in a circle as most occult symbols.

THE ZODIAC

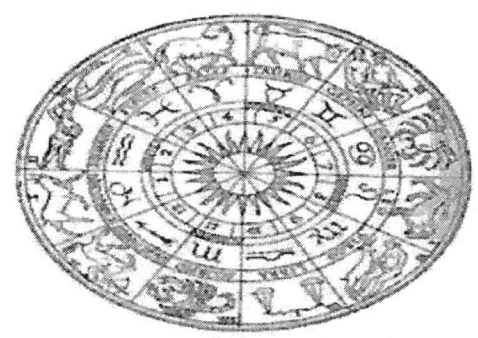

The zodiac is used in occult satanic adoration. The practitioners know their god as Baal or Lucifer. This includes the horoscopes signs.

In astrology, the zodiac constellations define twelve zodiac signs utilized historically as a method of divination and confession of horoscopes. The sign presents the date of birth linked to the being that was born that day, "branding" him for life.

The zodiac is formed by 12 signs or by 14 constellations. According to eastern astrology, the persons born under a certain zodiac sign have a common personality and future, which depends on their sign.

The problem with who believes in astrology is that his faith is in something empty, something hollow, and worst yet, in something condemned by God's word. Note what it is said in God's word about astrology in Jeremiah 10:2:

"Thus saith the Lord, Learn not the way of the heathen, and be not dismayed at the signs of heaven; for the heathen

are dismayed at them"

There are people who if the horoscope says that they will have a good day, this person will leave their house with a positive mind, but if the horoscope says they will have a bad day, this person will leave their house feeling depressed and defensive, waiting for the worst to happen.

People will do well in submitting to God's word and banish astrology and horoscope from their lives.

Chapter V: Origins of some festivities

I would like to show you some origins of some festivities that are commonly celebrated. There are some that unite us and let us share with our families, friends and brothers in Christ, like Christmas. It is a time to share and give presents and gifts and love; although love should be a prevailing concept throughout all year. Even though we know that December 25th was a date that Christ was not born, we can retain much of doing things and preach, attract the unconverted, say that Christ incarnate and was born to give salvation because He loves human kind. I do not believe that God has called people and churches to steal photos from Facebook pages from other people and churches to form gossip and accuse them of "apostates" just because they put Christmas lights in their churches and do activities to preach Christ. Christians do not worship any "pagan god" to be Christmas. For the Christian, Christ is Christmas and to some, it's just business and expenses. It is excellent to gain knowledge about things, but at the same time, to be balance is very important. Those who do not really celebrate Christmas, birthdays or don't give blood transfusion even if their child dies are the Jehovah's Witnesses.

PASSION WEEK

Before eggs could be associated with Passion Week (Easter), they were worshiped in many spring festival rituals. The Romans, the Gallic, Egyptians, Chinese and Persians all worshiped eggs as a universal symbol. Since ancient times, they were painted and worshiped.
In pagan times, they represented the "rebirth" of the earth, since according to them, after winter had passed; the earth was miraculously reborn as an egg full of life. These eggs were buried under the foundations of buildings, to protect for evil. Also, pregnant young woman carried an egg with them in order to "strengthen the sex of their soon to be born babies". Also, there is a Polish legend that says that when Mary Magdalene went to the tomb to anoint Jesus' body, she carried with her a basket full of eggs which served as food. When she

arrived to the tomb, she uncovered the eggs and found that they were miraculously painted with rainbow colors.

In ancient Babylon, there was a religious international festivity in which it was celebrated the birth of Semiramis, or Ishtar. She had also falsely said that she had lived as a spirit before the flood with Noah, and that she had descended inside a great egg which fell into the Euphrates River. The goddess on the egg of Ishtar (Easter egg) was Semiramis under another name. The name "Easter" is pronounced as the same as "Ishtar", thus "Easter Egg" means "Istar's Egg". This celebration celebrated the birth of Semiramis on Thursday, Good Friday and Sunday of Resurrection. It was changed by the death and resurrection of Christ. Some say that the Resurrection Sunday, with its ancient services done on sunrise, is entirely pagan. From this is where the "mysticism" is derived, which states that Attis (who was considered to be the only god, both as Father and Son) came to earth, and was killed in a log and sent to hell on a Friday, and resurrected on a Sunday. Some say this is the origin of the Easter holiday, and it's not the same as Jesus Christ being sacrificed on Passover.

THE ORIGIN OF CHRISTMAS

The Bible does not mention anywhere the date that Jesus Christ was born; it could have been around the Feast of Tabernacles, which was held between September and October, in what was known as the period of 8 to 5 BCE (Before the Common Era) The 25th of December was a difficult time for the shepherds to be out in the open with their sheep (Luke 2:8-20), since there were no sheep in the field for that time of year. And besides, the Bible states that it was a very cold and rainy year in that geographic area, since it was the ninth month of the lunar calendar.

Time after Constantine issued the edict of tolerance to Christian persecution, at the Council of Nicaea, on 325 AD., was declared the divinity of Jesus and was agreed to establish a "nativity", during the boreal solstice, which is when the sun is farthest from the Ecuador, the shortest day of the year in the northern hemisphere.

The word nativity comes from the Latin 'nativitas', which means "birth", and the word "Christmas" comes from the old English "Cristes Maesse" which means "Mass of Christ". At that time, this date coincided with a very important agricultural and solar festive period for the Roman Empire. It was a very popular pagan festival that was established between 273 and 274 BC by the emperor Aurelian in honor to the arrival of the solstice birth of the "invincible sun": the "Natalis Solis Invicti". The priests agreed to maintain the popular pagan festival but changing everything to a religious "mask" that replaces the birth of Jesus. For the year 1100, Christmas had become the most "religious" festivity of all Europe.

To go even further into ancient times, the 25th of December was celebrated in Egypt as the birth of the solar gods. A brother and a lover to Isis, Osiris, would be a beneficent god, whose birth was announced by a mysterious and powerful voice that echoed in the Temple of Thebes, according to Egyptian mythology. In ancient Babylon, it was the date in which Tammuz (Semiramis' son) was born. Initially, she and her followers argued that on the 25th of December an evergreen tree sprouted during the night of a dry stump in Babylon, and that Nimrod (who had already died) would secretly return every year at the same time to leave presents on the tree.

December was the tenth month according to the Roman calendar, which is where its name comes from. The celebrations of this month were honored to Saturn. They were celebrated from the 17 to the 23 of December, which constituted a week. The habit of the candles and Christmas lights comes from the people of small resources that received thin wax candles from their superiors, which according to tradition, they used to them to drive away the gods of thunder, storm and tempest, as well as witches and evil spirits, for which they were tied to a sacred oak.

Santa Claus, or Saint Nicholas, comes from the German and Dutch folklore, in which a person known as Nikolaos of Myra, who was a bishop of Lisinia (Asia Minor). Legend says that he took his salary of three years and that every year he made a ball of gold that he rolled over the houses of the poor. One of those balls had rolled over stocking or sock. From there comes the tradition of receiving candy or gifts in these Christmas stockings. These three balls of gold were a symbol that the merchants later used, thus, Saint Nicholas was transformed in the "saint" of commerce.

In Holland, Santa Claus was known as Sinterklass, who was the patron saint of the city of Amsterdam. His origin is based on the god Woden, from the word "Wednesday" comes from, which means "the day of Woden". This mythological character was described as somebody that traveled riding on a white horse, dressed with floating robes, and had a white beard, a great hat and had a book in his hand. The aspect of Santa Claus as a comical fat character dressed in red emerged XIX century. The colors red and green were used for ancient pagan cults. The ivy was sacred to the god Attis, and her priests had it tattooed on their skin. The mistletoe was sacred for the Druids and the Aryans. The ivy and the mistletoe are red and green.

HALLOWEEN

We should all avoid celebrating this day. Many Christians celebrate it without knowing where it came from. I want to tell you that it's exceedingly impossible to separate Halloween from the druids. They were the originators of this demonic celebration. We know through history that the Celtics lived in what we know today as France, Scotland, Ireland, Germany and England. The Celtic priests were called druids, whom later were defeated and conquered by the Romans.

What is known of them today is through Romans, Greeks and Irish documents, which agree in their information since knowledge of the Druids was never written, but transmitted by word of mouth from generation to generation among themselves. Throughout the years they had hidden their traditions. However Davies, a writer form the XVI century, that studied his family line, discovered that he was a descendant of druid priests that fought against Caesar. He could clearly describe the human sacrifices that his ancestors performed and the secret sacrifices that still took place by the druids of his time, for which he received much criticism of his family for writing this information.

As for the Romans and Greeks writings, these date back to 200 years B.C. They described extensively the barbaric human sacrifices that the druid priests did. As for the Irish writings, they specify little about the sacrifices and talk with more detail about the magic that these people performed to cause storms, curse places, create magical obstacles and kill with spells.

It wasn't until the year 47 B.C., when Rome finally defeated the druids and human sacrifices were banned. The few remaining priests went to hiding. For the day that Halloween is celebrated, which is the 31st October, was when the druids priests celebrated these human sacrifices for the purpose of honoring their sun god (Baal), and to Samhain, Lord of the dead. According to their beliefs, the sinful souls of those who had died during the year, were in a place of torment and could only be liberated if they pleased Samhain with cruel sacrifices. The Irish records tell of how fascinated the catholic monks were by the druids, who soon became important members of their monasteries.

It was Pope Gregory the Great who decided to incorporate the holiday of the druids to the Catholic Church. Later, Pope Gregory III moved the festivity from October 31st to November 1st and named it "All Saints' Day". Pope Gregory IV decreed this day to be observed by the universal church. For this reason, Halloween is a name that derives "All Hallows Eve".

The founders of the United States of America, who were puritans, believers in the Lord, did not allow for that day to be celebrated because they knew its terrible pagan origin. It was around the year 1900 when Halloween was celebrated in a more general way in the U.S., since in the decade of 1840, a terrible potato shortage in Ireland caused the arrival of millions of Irish Catholics, who brought this practice with them. The tradition of going door to door with costumes and candies, comes from the druid belief that said that while the sinful and lost souls waited for their trial, Samhain set them free on earth for one night, which was the 31st October, and it was believed that these souls arrived together to the homes of people, who waited with a feast on the table. People were terrified of these spirits, since they believed that they could hurt or kill them if the sacrifices they offered did not please Samhain. This way, to keep the spirits away from their homes, they carved demonic faces on pumpkins and big turnips, and placed candles inside them. The tradition of collecting apples with the mouth and gifting nuts was a Roman addition to the druid new year's eve, since the Romans worshiped Pomona, who was goddess of the harvest, therefore they combined the celebration of Halloween with their harvest festival in honor to their goddess Pomona.

THE ORIGIN OF CARNAVAL
At the beginning of the middle Ages, the Catholic Church proposed a significance of carnival: the Vulgar Latin carne-levare, which meant 'to abandon the flesh' (which precisely was the mandatory requirement for all the people during all the Fridays of Lent). But it did not make sense that precisely the word carnival means the prohibition of the festivals (in which meat and bacon were always eaten).
After that, another etymology surged which it's the one that is currently managed in the popular sphere: The Italian word 'carnavale' would mean that during carnival season "meat is permitted", therefore it can be eaten. But in the late twentieth century, various authors started to suspect the pagan origin of this name. Carna is the Celtic goddess of beans and bacon. It would also be connected to indo-European festivals dedicated to the god Karna (who in the Mahabharata appears as a human being, and is the eldest brother of the Pandavas, and son of the Sun god and queen Kunti). Currently the carnival has become a popular celebration of playful character. A carnival is, well, a public celebration that combines elements like costumes, parades and street parties. Carnival also refers to a specific date, which is held after Christmas and which concludes on the Tuesday of carnival, which is the last Tuesday before the start of the catholic Lent. The carnival period is also known by the French term of mardi gras, 'fatty Tuesday' or of the fat (bacon). During Lent the catholic canons indicate that no one should eat meat, but fish and vegetables. After the Carnaval, it can continue "over" Lent, denominating itself with the French term "Mi Caréme".

Chapter VI: Deceptions of the Enemy and some prophetic fulfillment

THE NEW AGE

The god of this false religion is an impersonal god, since it's not more that the person's "interior energy". They establish that only our ego is capable of facing the paradox of modern times, in which science and technology has not solved the fundamental problems of man.

The New Age intends to try to reconcile that which is contradictory: The personal God, Almighty (Christianity) and the "energy" god which is confused with the matter, which comes from pantheism, which is the doctrine that identifies the universe with God, but whose reflection must begin with an understanding of the divine reality and then speculate on the relationship between the divine and not divine.

This religion is made to suit the consumer, since it's a mixture of religious elements, which is attractive to men to try to satisfy the spiritual necessity, which we know that only God can fulfill, all for the purpose of feeling good without recognizing God's sovereignty and being submitted to His perfect will, which implies denying ourselves and let die the old creature, so that the new spiritual creature is born.

This religion is more emotional than doctrinal. It's something based on a disorder without any type of subjection or divine logic. There are advertisements of New Age books that offer the correct handling of ancestral knowledge like yoga, Feng Shui, and that meditation will control and equilibrate the energies and develop all latent potential.

The devil knows that to create a lie that convinces and confuses, has to be mixed with the truth. Because of this the Bible condemns spiritual lukewarmness. Notice that the New Age talks about a god that understands us and accepts us as we are, which corresponds to an attribute of our real God, but in difference, that their god does not require conversion, does not compromise with us nor does he expect any commitment from us.

This is something serious, besides that man is put in God's place, since they establish that man self-realization and its christification, will be archived without the intermediation of any religious organization.

This means that the believer of this lie "christifies" himself, since it does not need Jesus Christ. This being said, we can then see that Christ is not for them the savior of the world that gave His life to redeem our sins on the cross.

In the New Age, Jesus is reduced to an obsolete teacher of an old "surpassed" religion, for which they believed they have surpassed Christ. They believe themselves capable in their own understanding of the "spiritual auto-realization" and to enter into the "holistic" culture, which is a mix of different religions, which is an old arrogance that marked **gnosticism.**

The New Age does not possess any type of hierarchy, it does not have any direction or any type of structural order, nor does it possess any dogmas, which tells us that it does not possess any fundamental truth or any constructive lifestyle. For this reason it is so attractive to modern man, since it represents the birth of a new conscience, a type of "mental aperture of tolerance", fraternity, reconciliation, and a new way to see and live life.

When the Antichrist is ruling, there will be a universal religion. Precisely, the new age tries to unify all religions, making a synthesis and choosing from each one of them what they best see fit. This posture, that has gained much height in our modern world, is not something new, it is very much established in our present time, but since long ago similar ideas had existed that has wanted to impersonate Jesus.

When we talk about the New Age, we talk about an unfounded disaster, in which man himself establishes its own truths, and its own means to "auto-realization", we can say what has been already said of Marxism: "All the good that it has is not good, and all the new that it has is not good".

"Woe unto them that call evil good, and good evil; that put darkness for light, and light for darkness; that put bitter for sweet, and sweet for bitter! Woe unto them that are wise in their own eyes, and prudent in their own sight!" (Isaiah 5:20-21)

G-12 OR GOVERNMENT OF THE TWELVE

Unlike the New Age, or any sect, G-12 is more dangerous, since it's a movement that is located inside some denominational churches, like: the Pentecostal, Assemblies of God, Charismatic, Disciples of Christ, Mission Board, etc. Some churches have accepted the G-12 method as a modern strategy to grow faster and more "efficiently" the congregation. The foundation of this movement is structured; firstly it is two organized events: meeting of the same sex and age; and the famous "encounters". These are held once a month with new people and that have embraced this vision for quite some time. They claim that the Christian believer can only be liberated from internal struggles by attending these meetings. This is wrong, since it is based on something that goes by works and not by faith. According to them, salvation is achieved through: repentance, inner healing and breaking curses. But when you repent you have to specify: the time, place and date, and the individuals where, on what and with who you sinned. If we analyze this, it is something that goes according to the limitation of the human mind; but not goes according to the infinite capacity of God to forgive. Salvation comes by His grace when there's genuine repentance from the person, the latter renouncing to sin. This involves a change of thought which in turn leads to a change of action.

In other aspects, within its basic teachings, success is a foundation philosophy; they establish a "success stair" which is based in four concepts: win, consolidate, discipling and sending. As soon as the newly converted accepts the new vision they begin to disciple in this direction and they prepare him to go out and win others to the new vision.

The role of the "pre-encounters" is to prepare the persons to arrive and participate of the "encounters" with a "free" mind without prejudice or ties to the "old" concepts. It is nothing but a weekend away from the individual's community, family and church, which is practically the same as the spiritual retreats of the Jesuits of the Opus Dei.

It is also intended, that the newly converted develops in a very short time, which is approximately three months. The newly converted has not even read the Pentateuch, but already knows all the G-12 concepts and then, he is already prepared to be a leader of twelve other people. It means that the very Word of God has less importance.

This model, based exclusively in the number 12, is only a personal interpretation, since the number seven stands out more, also that there are other numbers with meaning and symbolism that cannot be denied or ignored.

To make you understand, what I mean is that the number 12 means government perfection. Many theologians affirm that Jesus Christ could have chosen that number among those who would be His apostles, because it prefigures the perfect government that will be established by Him in His second coming, since only God will be able to carry out the perfect government in His second coming. Twelve (12) is product of three (3), which is the perfectly divine and heavenly number, and also from the number four (4), the earthly, the number that derives from all the material and the organic. This way, it is known theologically, that it's the Trinity (3) government over the Earth (4). If then the number 12 is characteristic of the apostles, by whom the G-12 are driven by, then, who is Jesus Christ? Is it them?

"Little children, it is the last time: and as ye have heard that antichrist shall come, even now are there many antichrists; whereby we know that it is the last time. They went out from us, but they were not of us; for if they had been of us, they would no doubt have continued with us: but they went out, that they might be made manifest that they were not all of us" (1 John 2:18-19)

ANGEL WORSHIPPING

I have had the privileged opportunity to see angels in my room by beautiful experiences the Lord gave me. I was able to see their silhouettes with my eyes closed, and feel them praying for me and minister me before the church service and crusades.

In one occasion, waking up really early in the morning, I saw a little angel that was over my computer's printer. He looked at me with great tenderness and love. Upon seeing him, I instinctively felt scared, but suddenly I felt peace and relief that calmed me while watching him. Before seeing him materializing before my eyes, I saw how blue phosphorescent lines that intertwined to then show him to me. I remember that his eyes were like flames that the fire emits when it's burning, but color blue.

Before beginning God's call, when I was seventeen, I remember feeling an angel and then hear him singing while he was playing a harp at the same time. My soul came out of my body and elevated almost touching the ceiling, over the bed. I saw Jesus Christ, the visible form of God, strolling around while I once was washing my car when I was nineteen, just a little time before I started to preach when I was twenty years old. I have also seen Him interceding for me in a same place, in my room, but banishing and reappearing again in various positions of praying (on His knees, standing up with His hands raised, etc.) showing me His omnipresence.

One time I also felt how he hugged me while I was sleeping, and pulled me back from my soul and spirit.

For God's glory I was able to understand through these graceful experiences His calling to my life. But I know how to differentiate between angels and demons, between Satan and God. I also know the purpose of the angels and God's attributes, which many do not understand, remembering also that demons were once also beautiful angels, but their sin corrupted their appearance. I have had also the opportunity to see them. They generally have the appearance of horrible reptiles and with faces of like a dead person or elves. Demons are

nothing else those fallen angels in the service of him who they chose as eternal master: Satan, who persuaded them and deceived them to follow him into a rampant battle against Jesus Christ to usurp His throne.
Satan in his rebellion forgot that he is nothing more than a created being, the same as all the angels of heaven, and that God was the one who covered him with infinite majesty.
From here we can understand that every angel, as a created being, not worthy of being worshipped. The only one to who should be worshipped, honored and praised is God. Today it exist a false doctrine of "communicating with one's angel". The devil, by all means, seeks to steal what is our purpose with God, which is to serve, obey, worship Him, for which is obtained through the communication with Him when we pray.
Jesus Christ is the only one to which we should claim to, and through whom me can reach the Father so that the Holy Spirit our great Comforter be the one to undertake or carry out his work, Jesus is the only mediator between God and man (1 Timothy 2:5), the only one who we should claim to, not to a certain angel, either cherub or seraph, or an archangel or from any other angelical hierarchy, since Christ, as Son of God, is superior to the angels.
"Hath in these last days spoken unto us by his Son, whom he hath appointed heir of all things, by whom also he made the worlds; Who being the brightness of his glory, and the express image of his person, and upholding all things by the word of his power, when he had by himself purged our sins, sat down on the right hand of the Majesty on high; Being made so much better than the angels, as he hath by inheritance obtained a more excellent name than they." (Hebrews 1:2-4)
It is a very regrettable fact that even within the churches, despite all the biblical teachings, there are believers that give more importance to angels that to God himself. This can be expressed in two ways: consciously or unconsciously.
Angel's posses certain attribute. First of all, as we have said, they were created by God, like us (Psalms 33:6). Because of this, we cannot worship them and take them into account more that the one who created them, which is God. Angels are also ministering spirits in favor to those

of us who accepted Christ (Hebrews 1:14), and are also placed by God as our fellow servants (Revelation 22:9)

Apart from all their power, and from us being slightly smaller than them, angels should not be revered or worshiped since they are not gods, and do not act or do anything until God orders them to (Psalms 8:5), also that they do not stop glorifying the name of God, whereby day and night they claim:

"And one cried unto another, and said, Holy, holy, holy, is the Lord of hosts: the whole earth is full of his glory." (Isaiah 6:3)

If they know God's sovereignty, and are placed by God to our favor, how is it possible that we should worship them? Many misrepresent the prerogatives of the Angel of God in the Old Testament, since this angel could give blessings (Genesis 48:16), was as if God himself was speaking (Genesis 22:12), and only this angel could receive worship and do so in the name of the Lord (Joshua 5:13-15). But it was because it was one of the representations of our Lord Jesus Christ here on earth before his incarnation, whereby many theologians also agree.

As an example, we see part of the story of Jacob. An angel gave him the name of Israel, which means "the one who fights with God or God fights", "Because he have fought with God and with men and have won." (Genesis 32:28), because of the blessing he fought for, not letting the angel go until he blessed him, so the angel dislocated the lace on his thigh with just touching him. Jacob called this place "Peniel" which means "the face of God", "for seeing God face to face" (Genesis 32:20). This angel or "male" was Jesus Christ, the visible form of God.

In this modern time, more than ever, we have to be very careful with "apparition" of angels. Notice that they are part of the history of many sects, such as the Mormonism and Islam. Remember that the evil one can even transfigure to an "angel of light", of which the apostle Paul warns us about (2 Corinthians 11:14).

I don't means with this that all the apparitions of angels are going to be false; but that as the Bible says: **"But though we, or an angel from heaven, preach any other gospel unto you than that which we have preached unto you, let him be accursed." (Galatians 1:8).**

HOROSCOPE SIGNS

Astrology is the study of the influence of the stars in the destiny and the behavior of men. It is also known as **uranoscopy**. It is a very ancient practice. Remember that in the beginnings of idolatry, of which we already discussed, Nimrod and Semiramis, in ancient Babylon, initiated it, also, when Europe was uninhabited and uncultivated, the Sumerians and Babylonians have already found themselves searching the answer to their desires in heaven. Note the astrologers of the court of Nebuchadnezzar (Daniel 2:2). The astrologers sustain that the position of the stars in the exact moment of a person's birth and their subsequent movements, reflect the character and destiny of this person. They also perform, astral cards also called horoscopes that situate the position of the stars in a given moment, like a person's birth, for example, from them they give to their conclusions about the individual's future. In an astrological card is placed what is called the ecliptic, the Sun's apparent annual path across the sky, with the twelve sections that receive the name of the zodiac sign, which are Aries, Taurus, Gemini, Cancer, Leo, Virgo, Libra, Scorpio, Sagittarius, Capricorn, Aquarius and Pisces. To each planet (including the Sun and the Moon) it is given a particular sign depending on the location of the ecliptic in which it appears that planet and in the moment that the horoscope is made. Each planet represents basic human tendencies. When the astrologers mention or name a person by a determined sign, they are referring to the solar sign of that person;

this is, the sign that the Sun occupied in the moment of his birth. We cannot confuse astrology with astronomy, since astronomy is the science that has as an objective treat the constitution, the relative position and the movement of the stars and planets; by the contrary, the astrology is a false science that only seeks to push people away from God and steal money from the unwary who want to know their future. Our Lord Jesus Christ, when he accused the scribes and Pharisees, he called them "generation of snakes" and "whitewashed tombs", since they appeared to be pious but inside were full of all kinds of filth and that they were no more than rapacious wolves (Luke 3:7; Matthew 23:25). For that time Caiaphas, which was high priest, together with Annas, his father in-law, were who governed Jerusalem under the direction of Rome, they also handled the corrupt religious machinery of that time. They were members of secret societies that they practiced what it is known as the Kabbalah, which was a type of mystical interpretation of the Sacred Scriptures. It was a system of occult techniques used even today by some rabbis, to analyze the Sacred Scriptures and communicate with evil spirits. It is believed that this was originated in the deportation of Jews to Babylon. Jesus Christ knew of their occult practices and their lack of mercy against the poor and widows, that's why they were condemned by Him. The same way, He also condemns in our times this type of mystical, or astral, or occult practices. Christ is the answer for everything. I have seen Christians that I know consult with horoscopes from newspapers or magazines, or wait for it anxiously on the television to "know" what their future hold, saying also that there is nothing wrong with consulting this type of false source.

The objective of astrology (which is nothing more than pseudoscience) is to separate from the true knowledge that God gives us through His Word, since the Bible has the answers to all our questions. We should not be anxious for our future or fear for the same, since our life is hidden in Christ (Colossians 3:1-3) and our path is in the hands of God (Psalms 37:5). Consulting with horoscopes signs is sin, since it values more the creation than the Creator. God made the stars and planets so they could function in the celestial mechanics (Jeremiah 31:35-36), besides that astrology is a lie, which the same Nebuchadnezzar discovered when he had a dream that none of his astrologers could interpret or tell (Daniel 2:8-9).

These persons only tell lies and things that are obvious to separate people from the truth and to fatten their pockets. This activity, like all sin, is addictive until it completely destroys you. There are people who become addictive to the consultation of horoscopes and that for anything that those signs say, they can either become glad or depressed, or cause them panic. It is something without foundation that produces various moods in the life of who clings to this. God prohibits this practice.

"If there be found among you, within any of thy gates which the Lord thy God giveth thee, man or woman, that hath wrought wickedness in the sight of the Lord thy God, in transgressing his covenant, And hath gone and served other gods, and worshipped them, either the sun, or moon, or any of the host of heaven, which I have not commanded" (Deuteronomy 17:2-3)

I want you to know that worshiping the stars does not only mean kneeling down before them, but to consult them through horoscopes, since you are giving it the place that belongs to God. Only God knows our future and only to Him we pray for the decisions that we're about to take so that it is Him who shows us.

King Saul, of Israel, according to the Bible, was rejected by God for disobeying Him and meet the people's favor rather than the divine order (1 Samuel 15:23). But it was the fact of consulting a psychic what determined his definitive death that led him to hell, since he ended up killing himself (1 Samuel 28:3-25, 31:1-6).

When the Bible tells us about the "Wise men" (Matthew 2:1-12), that cannot be interpreted as if they were astrologers. They were a group of gentile scholars they knew perfectly well that the birth of the Messiah would be announced by the appearance of an extraordinary star. This shows us without any doubt, that the information of the birth of the Savior of the World spread through the oriental intellectual class. The prophet Daniel, who was the chief of the wise men in Babylon, could have spread the news about the prophecy of the star of Jacob through the intellectual class of Babylon and Persia (Daniel 4:9).

When the Bible mentions Belteshazzar "master of the magicians", it was the name given to Daniel by a culture that called everything magic. We all know that Daniel's wisdom was coming from the only and real God. Daniel NEVER was involved in the arts of magic or astrology, and the wise men that went to visit Jesus when He was born, were wise astronomers that studied the sky from a real divine perspective. Daniel repudiated the magic and astrology of the Chaldeans, and served only and exclusively the true God.

ALIENS AND UFOS
The subject of aliens and unidentified flying object, which the acronym is UFO, is something that is continually grows in our modern society. Those of us who know the Word do not allow ourselves to be confused, since we know that they are demonic entities in a tangible form. An alien is any being that is or belongs to another place in the universe other than the planet Earth. Precisely, fallen angels are beings that after their rebellion against God, He cast them out from the kingdom of heaven to the space next to Satan. Obviously they are non-terrestrial beings, with greater knowledge, and even with powers. Obviously these are corrupted powers that are part of the kingdom of darkness.

Some movies constantly prepare us for things before they happen. An example of this is the continuing films that Hollywood started to release in the 90's about the end of the world, because it was believed that in the year 2000 everything would end, besides that there was a prophecy about this by the famous Nostradamus. After the attacks of September 11, 2001, it also began to make war films to prepare society for the war that North America was going to have against terrorism.

Regarding UFOs, many have testified to having seen these spaceships or flying saucers, even some having certain experiences with these beings from other worlds. This we have seen in movies and television series. In 1982, Michael London, from "Los Angeles Times" newspaper, gathered a group of eight people that had experienced encounters with UFO and aliens for a special presentation of the movie "E.T.", by Stephen Spielberg. This group of people stated that "it was about a real movie, and not some romance", and that also it was part of a preparation process for the arrival of aliens to Earth. They said the movie was a way to invite the population to have less fear of the paranormal and that the kids were precisely the place to start, since "everything was done through them".

These beings are generally described in movies as identical to us in many aspects, more intelligent and advanced in what refers to technology, friendly beings to live in peace and to have the capacity of teaching things to us, and that supposedly only care about our interests. The "aliens" use normal New Age terminology when they communicate to the persons that they choose. The best example of this is their teachings that state that they are the "ascended masters of the hierarchy", and that they are preparing again to intervene in world history to lead humanity to a much broader level in terms of conscience. They state that they would choose a human and that they would give him powers and superhuman knowledge (does it remind you of what Nimrod used to say in ancient times?), and that this human would lead them to a global government and world peace [UFO: End Time Disillusion, David Lewis, p.46].

We can see here a coincidence between what the "spirit guides" that the New Age writers claim to have are saying and what the aliens are saying to their "contacted", with the purpose of re-directing everything towards the New World Order. The New Age seeks to abolish all government established, the same as the aliens according to what is testified by those that had experiences with these beings, also they both seek to abolish all religions and combine them into one, and establish a one-world government.

It has been proved, that without an exception, every person claiming having contact with extraterrestrial beings, had previous connection with some metaphysical activity or with sects related to Satanism, witchcraft, psychic phenomena, New Age, canalization, etc.

Satan's goal has always been the lie, starting with making the world believe that neither he nor the demons exist, in order to further deceive mankind. The enemy has always wanted that humans only believe through what their five senses tells them to get the approval that something exists, the opposite of what it is faith, which is to believe in

what cannot be seen (Hebrews 11:1). Satan proceeds to make man believe that if something works, then it must be consequently true. This way, humans become more susceptible to demonic activity and are incapable of perceiving spiritual deception that will slowly lead them to condemnation. This way aliens and UFO phenomena begin to appear more frequently and make contact with people. By not believing that the devil and the demons exist, then they give them attention when they materialize in any form and with claim to be from outer space with theories and falsehoods that contradict the Bible. By showing themselves as superior beings, of technology, and "advanced" religion, they pretend to make us forget Christianity and to obey them instead. There are Christian authors who have written the idea that the demons will manifest themselves physically on earth, in the eyes of all mankind, as aliens and arriving in armadas of spaceships, to which they attribute the passage of chapter 9 of Revelation, that talks about demons that are released from the abyss. Resembling locusts to Apostle John, they will invade the Earth to torment all of those who are not saved, and their leader is Abaddon or Apollyon. The similarity in this case, is that the study of New Age refers to these beings as "illuminated leaders of the New Age".
Satan has always been constantly moving to manipulate world events and to reach a global economy, government and religion, which is almost complete. These aliens are nothing else than demons to which God has permitted to physically manifest themselves and make signs in the heavens because we are in the end of times.

The problem is that today there are many Christians do not possess a solid understanding about the reality of demons, and are susceptible to any deception. We see constantly that the media is trying to prepare us for the arrival of these extraterrestrial beings.

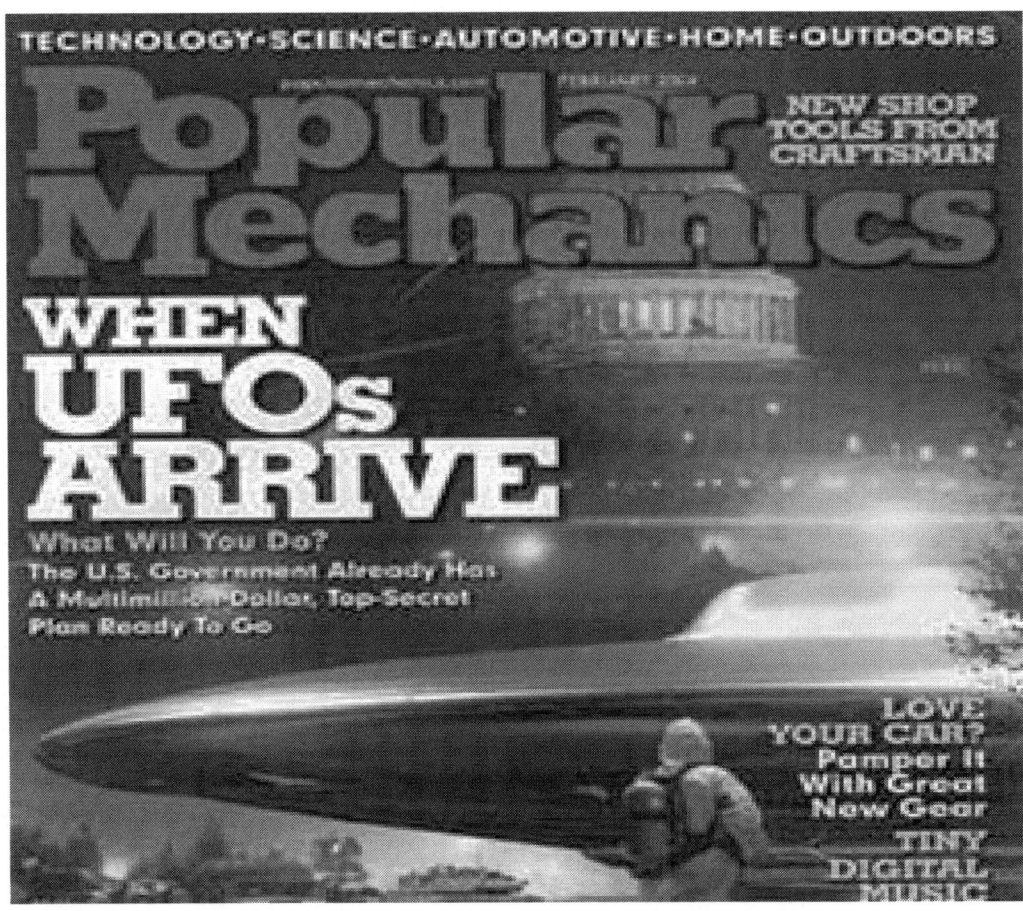

My intention with this is not to write science fiction, but to compare those facts from a biblical perspective and what the other Christian authors have claimed.

The book of Revelation talks to us about the battle between the archangel Michael and his angels against the Dragon and the angels that are from the Dragon, which is Satan and his demons (Revelation 17:7-12), to which Michael beats and throws from the second heaven, which is space, to earth in the middle of the Great Tribulation.

The lost Gospel of Judas

Another deception that the devil has put today to continue to keep in its continuing effort to discredit the Bible, is called "The lost gospel of Judas", which the media has taken the task of reporting. This was a book that was lost about two millenniums ago that reappeared a while ago on a copy in Coptic discovered in Egypt. According to this work, Judas was the only one who knew the true identity of Jesus and collaborated in the divine plan of the sacrifice of the Only Begotten Son of God, to whom the Master had commissioned the most difficult mission: surrender him to his executioners.

The volume consists of 66 pages with leather cover and papyrus paper that some looters found in the 70's in some caves near Minya and that was around for 30 years without anyone checking its authenticity or translating it.

After having survived 1,600 years, thanks to the dry climate of the dessert, it almost became powder after spending 16 years inside a security box in the cost of New York State, in the humid environment of Long Island. On 2001 it was acquired by the Maecenas foundation which started its restoration process, to then enter into collaboration with National Geographic.

It was concluded to be a genuine book, due to screening tests of the Carbon 14 that proved to be written around 300 AD. Immediately it was scandalously reported that it was found a lost "gospel", and that the experts had "proved" that it was "real". What's interesting about the case is that they had not explained how this gospel totally contradicted all the other gospels of the Bible, and that it was genuine in terms of the year or age that it was written, but by the date on which it was finished, and of which it was proven as truthful, the Sacred Scriptures of the New Testament had already been entirely collected.

It is nothing but a writing of the Gnostics of Alexandria, in Egypt, that rejected the writings that were truly inspired by God. They considered themselves wise in their own opinion. Besides not believing in the New Testament, they always tried to discredit everything.

It is important that you know, to prevent any deceitful attack from the media or from any other source that the real Scriptures were in the hands of the true believers, but many fake books and gospels appeared around that period that contradicted the God's Word. At the time of the compilation of the New Testament, the Christians of the early church were carefully examining all the Gospels and classified them into three specific categories:

    1. Those that were universally accepted

    2. Those that were adulterated, as "The Acts of Paul", "The Shepherd of Hermas", the "Didache", the "Apocalypse of Peter" and "The Epistles of Barnabas".

    3. Those that were entirety false, as "The Gospel of Thomas", "The Gospel of Mathias", "The Acts of John" and "The Acts of Andrew".

    The books that today are in the real New Testament were subjected to the following analysis:

    1. If it was written by an apostle of Christ.

    2. If it possessed a high hierarchy of spiritual content.

    3. If it was universally accepted by all the congregations of the true church.

    4. If there was proof that the particular gospel had been a product of a divine inspiration, for which it was consider that the authority of the real writing is based on:

    A. The great Comforter that Jesus promised and that had arrived: The Holy Spirit.

B. The true believers had the gift of discernment.

C. The references that an author of the Bible makes of others. For example, Peter makes references of the writings of Paul as "Scriptures".

"And account that the long suffering of our Lord is salvation; even as our beloved brother Paul also according to the wisdom given unto him hath written unto you; As also in all his epistles, speaking in them of these things; in which are some things hard to be understood, which they that are unlearned and unstable wrest, as they do also the other scriptures, unto their own destruction." (2 Peter 3:15-16)

It is very easy to create a tabloid scandal that makes people go mad, like the case of Orson Welles in its radio program "The War of the Worlds" in 1938, by which he spread panic by being so realistic that many listeners truly believed that the Earth was being invaded by aliens. You need to have knowledge and not be fooled. For the time of the primitive church, there were many versions of Gnosticism which were all based in the same idea that "the material world was bad and was thus created by an inferior being". They had as a goal to escape from this "badly created" world to a purer and non-physical field of existence. This was the reason of which their interpretation of the Bible was distorted. The Gnostics blamed God for the problems and conditions of humankind, which actually the fault of Satan according to them. Therefore it can be said that they placed God in the place of Satan.

The lost gospel of Judas is nothing else than a Gnostic document that used the inversion of the relationship between Jesus and Judas to promote the Gnostic doctrine and it has limited historical data that does not pretend to be written by Judas.

Do not let yourself be deceived, the devil only wants to steal your faith.

THE DA VINCI CODE

This book, from its author Dan Brown, became a world phenomenon with more than 25 million of copies sold in almost all the world. Just like the "Lost Gospel of Judas" it became something to confuse and make people not believe in anything. The book "Da vinci Code" strongly attacks the Catholic Church as a church founded on pagan origins, which is true, but sets this religion as the one that has to be considered as "Christian", is false. Catholicism and Christianity is not the same thing. When we talk about Christianity, we are talking about something that is a hundred percent Christ-centered, which means that Jesus Christ is the center of everything, the Rock, the main stone and head angle of the Church (Matthew 21:42; Mark 12:10; Luke 20:17; Acts 4:11; Ephesians 2:20; 1 Peter 2:6). For the Roman Catholics and the Catholic Church, Peter was the first Pope, and they state that the church is founded in him and not in Jesus Christ because of the misinterpreted statement that Jesus Christ made to his apostle.

"And I say also unto thee, that thou art Peter, and upon this rock I will build my church; and the gates of hell shall not prevail against it." (Matthew 16:18)

Of the Greek translation, when Christ called his apostle: Peter, his name comes from the word "PETROS", which means "small pebble", and when He said "and upon this rock I will build my church", the word "rock "comes from the Greek word "PRETA", which is greater than a "small pebble", therefore Jesus Christ is the Rock. It is more than proven by all the above verses we have provided. Besides, the name "Simon", of the apostle Peter, means "sand" in Greek. Let see what Jesus says:

"Therefore whosoever heareth these sayings of mine, and doeth them, I will liken him unto a wise man, which built his house upon a rock (PETRA): And the rain descended, and the floods came, and the winds blew, and beat upon that house; and it fell not: for it was founded upon a rock. And every one that heareth these sayings of mine, and doeth them not, shall be likened unto a foolish man, which built his house upon the SAND: And the rain descended, and the floods came, and the winds blew, and beat upon that house; and it fell: and great was the fall of it." (Matthew 7:24-27)

The Vatican will be destroyed as well as all its followers. That's why God calls to get out of this system. Revelations 18:1-11 says:

"And after these things I saw another angel come down from heaven, having great power; and the earth was lightened with his glory.

[2] And he cried mightily with a strong voice, saying, Babylon the great is fallen, is fallen, and is become the habitation of devils, and the hold of every foul spirit, and a cage of every unclean and hateful bird.

[3] For all nations have drunk of the wine of the wrath of her fornication, and the kings of the earth have committed fornication with her, and the merchants of the earth are waxed rich through the abundance of her delicacies.

[4] And I heard another voice from heaven, saying, Come out of her, my people, that ye be not partakers of her sins, and that ye receive not of her plagues.

[5] For her sins have reached unto heaven, and God hath remembered her iniquities.

[6] Reward her even as she rewarded you, and double unto her double according to her works: in the cup which she hath filled fill to her double.

[7] How much she hath glorified herself, and lived deliciously, so much torment and sorrow give her: for she saith in her heart, I sit a queen, and am no widow, and shall see no sorrow.

[8] Therefore shall her plagues come in one day, death, and mourning, and famine; and she shall be utterly burned with fire: for strong is the Lord God who judgeth her.

⁹ And the kings of the earth, who have committed fornication and lived deliciously with her, shall bewail her, and lament for her, when they shall see the smoke of her burning,

¹⁰ Standing afar off for the fear of her torment, saying, alas, alas that great city Babylon, that mighty city! For in one hour is thy judgment come.

¹¹ And the merchants of the earth shall weep and mourn over her; for no man buyeth their merchandise anymore"

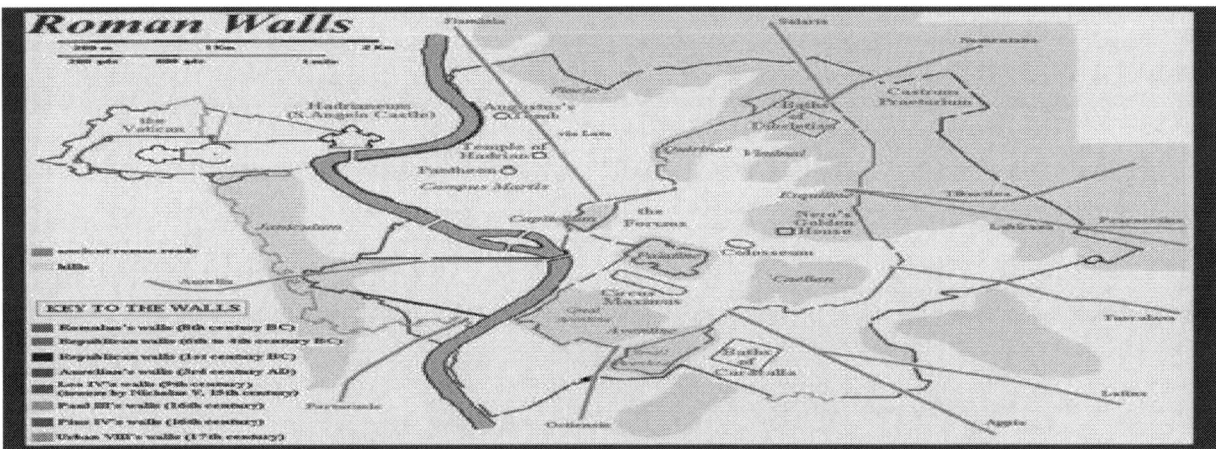

"And here is the mind which hath wisdom. The seven heads are seven mountains, on which the woman sitteth" (Revelation 17:9

The Da Vinci Code also shows Jesus Christ as any human being subjected to sins and weaknesses, and not how the Bible describes Him: THE SON OF GOD. It also presents that Jesus married Mary Magdalene and that he had sexual relationships with her and also had a daughter with her, stating that their descendants are with us today. This book says that Da Vinci was secretly Gnostic and pagan (something not proven), and that he expressed heretic ideas through subtle messages in his art, for which, is attributed to an interpretation of the painting of "The Last Supper", in which it is said that the individual seated at the right of Jesus, looks very feminine to be apostle John and they establish that it has to be a woman. It was also agreed, that in the figures of Jesus and this "woman", there is an "M".

Through his characters, Picknett and Prince, Dan Brown interprets that the person seated next to Jesus is Mary Magdalene, that the letter "M" that She and Jesus trace means "matrimony", and that when noticing that Da Vinci painted himself in painting facing the opposite direction of Jesus, says that he is rejecting the traditional interpretation. This is impossible to believe even to the experts in art history.

The true interpretation is that who is seated at the right of Jesus is really John. He is in a feminine aspect, because this was the historical way on Da Vinci's time, in which young men were represented, and also, Leonardo painted himself facing backwards, or to the opposite direction of Jesus to prove he was not worthy of Him. About the "M", it's just an interpretation that the devil has placed in the mind of this individual, creator of this book, "the Da vinci code", to discredit the Bible. Understand that Satan has been attacking the Bible for more than 1,500 years. This we just mention is only some of the follies of this book that besides Dan Brown, there cannot be another behind it that the lying devil himself.

THE VERICHIP

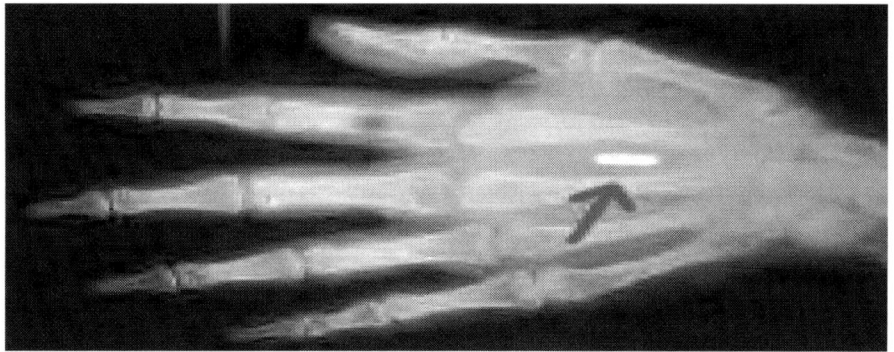

When we are told about a "mark" in the book of Revelations in the Bible, it doesn't mean that the Antichrist will literally come with a marker or ink to paint on the numbers 666 on the forehead or right hand to those who will decide to follow him. The Apostle John was describing everything that the Lord gave him according to his time. With a revelation of the future with Burger King, for example, he could not have described everything according to present time.

"And he causeth all, both small and great, rich and poor, free and bond, to receive a mark in their right hand, or in their foreheads: And that no man might buy or sell, save he that had the mark, or the name of the beast, or the number of his name. Here is wisdom. Let him that hath understanding count the number of the beast: for it is the number of a man; and his number is Six hundred threescore and six." (Revelation 13:16-18)

The company MOTOROLA was producing this microchip for MONDEX SMARTCARD, which developed various implants on humans using the bio-chip.
The bio-chip measures are 7mm long and 0.75mm wide, more or less like a rice kernel.
 It contains a transponder and a rechargeable Lithium battery. The battery is recharged by a thermocouple circuit that produces an electric current with the fluctuations of the body's temperature.

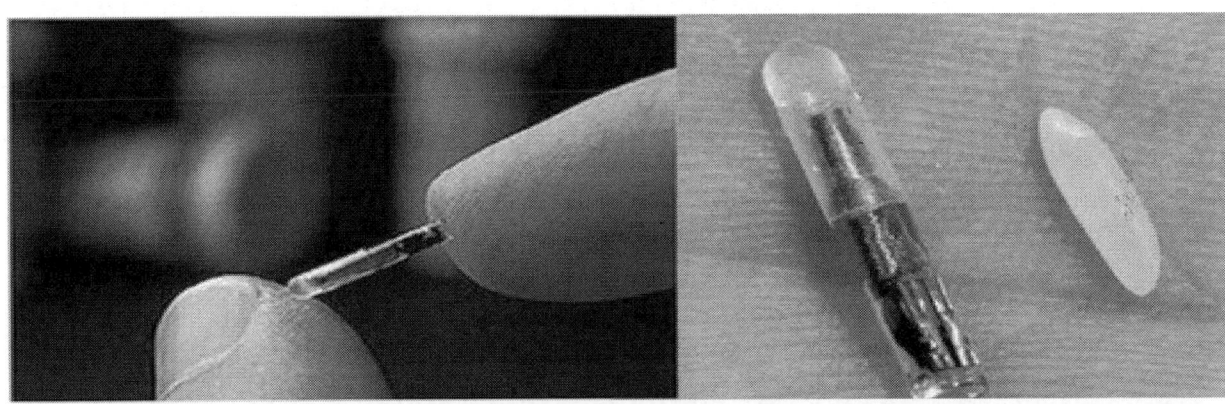

To define "transponder", IT IS A STORAGE AND INFORMATION READING SYSTEM IN A MICROCHIP, WHICH ITS READING OCCURS IN WAVES AS OF A REMOTE CONTROL.

They spent more than 1.5 million dollars in studies, only to know the best place to put this biochip in the human body. They found only two satisfactory and efficient places: the HEAD, under the scalp, and on the back of the hand, specifically the RIGHT HAND!
It was discovered that if the chip was inside a card, there would be serious problems. The chip could be cut off and information could be changed or falsified. Values could be altered, stolen or lost. There is only one solution to this problem, adopted by the company Motorola: the biochip implant on the right hand or on the head; where it could not be removed after the implant has been performed. If it was surgically extracted, the small capsule would break and the individual would be contaminated with Lithium, chemical content in micro battery, and then the Global Positioning System (by satellite) would detect if it was extracted, alerting the Police.

MONDEX means "Money on the right hand."
MON = Monetary - belonging to the money
DEX= DEXTER - belonging or located on the right hand

Project Director for microchip manufacturing disagreed initially with a rechargeable lithium biochip to be used for this because the breaking of capsule of the rechargeable lithium battery with body temperature was causing painful and ugly sores and ulcers.

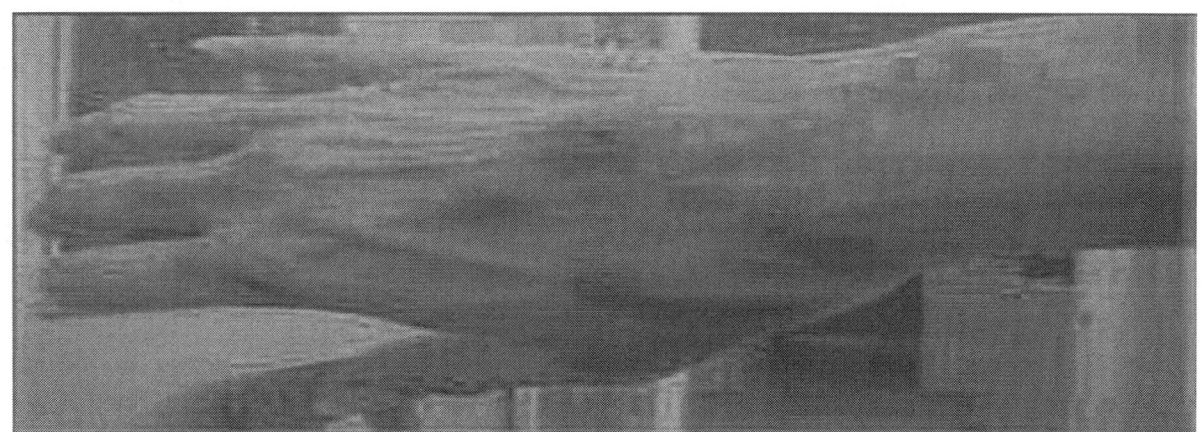

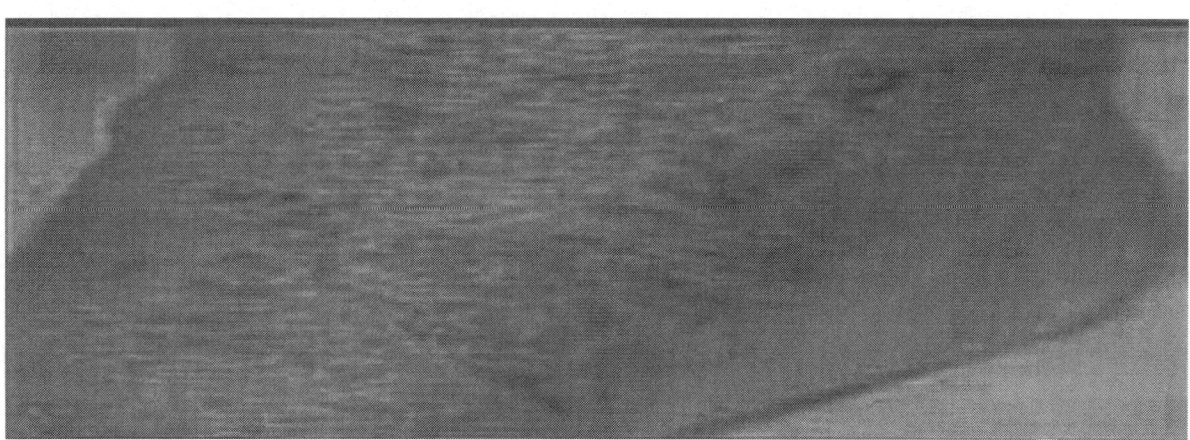

It is possible that the introduction of this verichip will exert some control over the person, preventing believing in the Messiah. The Bible condemns to eternal fire those who will have this mark.
"And the first went, and poured out his vial upon the earth; and there fell a noisome and grievous sore upon the men which had the mark of the beast, and upon them which worshipped his image" (Revelations 16:2)
"And the third angel followed them, saying with a loud voice, If any man worship the beast and his image, and receive his mark in his

forehead, or in his hand, The same shall drink of the wine of the wrath of God, which is poured out without mixture into the cup of his indignation; and he shall be tormented with fire and brimstone in the presence of the holy angels, and in the presence of the Lamb: And the smoke of their torment ascendeth up for ever and ever: and they have no rest day nor night, who worship the beast and his image, and whosoever receiveth the mark of his name." (Revelation 14:9-11)

I know this is the beginning of the technology that the Antichrist will use, but we can't say that this in present times is "the mark of the beast" already. The antichrist is not yet manifested on earth and this mark will be imposed three and a half years after rapture. The mark will have the name of the Antichrist. Do not accuse politicians or public figures to be the Antichrist.

No one will know who the Antichrist is until after the rapture. Pretend to know who the Antichrist is or will be, is like saying that you know when is going to happen the rapture and it is not known nor day nor hour. JUST LIKE THE BIBLE SAYS.

"And he said unto them, It is not for you to know the times or the seasons, which the Father hath put in his own power" (Revelation 16:2)

"<u>But of that day and hour no one knows,</u> not even the angels of heaven, but My Father only."But as the days of Noah were, so also will the coming of the Son of Man be (Matthew 24:36-37)

"Watch therefore, for you know neither the day nor the hour in which the Son of Man is coming." (Matthew 25:13)

True believers in God will not go through the Great Tribulation. One thing is the rapture and other Visible Second Coming of Christ to earth. No will ever know when the rapture is coming. However, according to the Bible we can know when will be the Second Visible Coming of Jesus Christ: AFTER 7 YEARS OF TRIBULATION.

The verichip is like a replacing for the barcode. Barcodes are symbols that can be read by machines and are made by patterns of black and white bars, and in some cases of chessboard-type square grids. There are different styles of barcodes. Code 39, UPC, and Code 128 are example of different styles. Inside these codes exists particles of information that are encoded within the barcode. The data are read by means of barcode scanners and they are generally used in conjunction with databases. Barcodes do not need human intervention, since they are read by automated machines and perform their function without the possibility of error. They can be used in any kind of merchandise for sale where it is digitalized at the cash register. Also, they are used in all sorts of shipping methods, labels, ID cards, propaganda sent by mail and bills.

All the lines, or bars, are associated with digital numbers in the bottom, except the marks at the beginning, middle and end. The three numbers which are omitted are three sixes.

Conclusion

It caught my attention a long time ago and article of a newspaper that I read about an Irish monk of the XII century named Malachy O'Morgan, who wrote a series of short Latin phrases that described, according to the prophetic vision he had, all the Popes that were going to be in the Vatican, until its complete disappearance, of which the Bible talks about on Revelation 18.

This book was written and drafted in the year 1139 and has 111 mottos, of which, one is for each Pope.

In the year 1144, the first Pope of which the revelation obtained, would be called "of the Tiber Castle". We see that from that chronological order, was Celestine II, born on a fort built over the Tiber River and was called "Tiberna".

Advancing drastically in this successive order of mottos, to the Pope Paul I, who only lasted 33 days, corresponds the motto "medietate lune", which means "half-moon". This Italian Pope's real name was Albino Luciani, which means "white light" or "the light that radiates half-moon".

To Pope John Paul II, Malachy wrote "De laboris solis" or "work of the sun", of which is known that this Pope was born in the same city that the astronomer Nicholas Copernicus, who created the heliocentric theory which states that Earth orbits around the Sun.

The Vatican was involved in a terrible scandal by Butler Pope Benedict XVI, who released to public terrible secrets of the Vatican. Part of the report brought to light said about homosexual relationships within the Vatican, and this was part of what led to the resignation of the last Pope. The News talked about it. This was an internal conspiracy within the Vatican for possible power struggles between Freemasons and Illuminati

The Phrase from Malachy, "Gloria Olivae", corresponds to Benedict XVI. Its means "glory of the olive". HE WAS PART OF THE OLIVETANS MONKS ORDER!

Lightning struck the basilica of San Pedro just after the resignation of the Pope

According to Malachy, there will be only one more Pope, with the motto "Petrus Romanus", who will not be buried in the Vatican, and will witness the end of the only city in the world surrounded by seven hills: Rome, which will be destroyed.

We are told about condemnation of the Vatican in Revelation, it is said: "And here is the mind which hath wisdom. The seven heads are seven mountains, on which the woman sitteth." (Revelation 17:9).

The current Pope, Francis, the first Latin-American Pope ever elected, took that name from **St. Francis of Assisi,** which his real name was Giovanni Bernardone Di Pietro. He was called "Di Pietro" because the name of his father was "Pietro Bernardone". Pietro means PETER.

The real name of the Pope is Jorge Mario Bergoglio. His last name is Italian. Italians come from the Romans. The translation of "PETRUS ROMANUS" means "PETER THE ROMAN"

God gives prophetic gifts to which He wills. If the prophecies are true, there is no reason to say no. Nebuchadnezzar was not a believer and God gave him a prophetic dream that Daniel interpreted it.

The truth is the Bible, but what we just show is pretty interesting

Be warm in the spirit, we don't know if immediately after you finish reading this book, or shortly afterwards, the Rapture arrives.
Do not stay here! We are close! Christ is coming soon! The end is near! Be prepared!

References

Bible reference from King James Version (KJV), Crown Copyright in UK

Illustrated dictionary of the Bible. Caribe Editorial, reproduction offices in Buenos Aires, Argentina, and San José, Costa Rica, Fifteenth edition, 1990, ISBN: 0-89922-033-9 ISBN: 0-89922-99-1.

Dictionary of Synonyms and Antonyms, Larousse Editorial, printed in Denmark, sixth reprint, 1995, ISBN: 2-03-800075-1.

Microsoft® Encarta® Encyclopedia 2000. © 1993-1999 Microsoft Corporation.

Maldonado, Guillermo. El Perdón, GM International, second edition, 2004, Miami, Florida, ISBN:1-59272-033-1.

Boza, Victor. El Espiritu Santo, Trujillo, Perú, 2003.

Maldonado, Guillermo. La Unción Santa, GM International, third edition, 2005, ISBN: 1-59272-003-X.

Hurlbut, Myles. Los Principios y el Poder de la Vision, Whitaker House, New Kingston, Pennsylvania, 2003, ISBN: 0-88368-965-0.

Hislop, Alexander. The Two Babylon's, Chick Publications, Ontario, CA, ISBN: 0-937958-57-3.

Chick, Jack. Cortinas de Humo, Chick Publications, Ontario, CA, 2004, ISBN: 0-937958-20-4.

Paris, Edmond. La Historia Secreta de los Jesuitas, Chick Publications, Ontario, CA 2006, ISBN: 0-7589-0628-5.

Godwin, Rick. Exponiendo La Hechicería En La Iglesia, Peniel Editorial, Buenos Aires, Argentina, 1998, ISBN: 987-9038-20-7.

Maldonado, Guillermo. La Liberación, El Pan De Los Hijos, GM International, first edition, 2001, Miami Florida, ISBN:1-59272-086-2.

Giberto, Antonio. Estudios Biblicos, "Cuando La Idolatria Amenaza La Iglesia De Cristo", Volume II #2, Patmos Editorial, Weston Florida.

Santos Medina, Jesús. Análisis Critico del Movimiento G12 y Sus Enseñanzas, análisis of four pages.

Chick, Jack. El Próximo Paso, Chick Publications, Ontario, CA, 1983, ISBN: 0-937958-15-8.

Muñoz Acebes, César. Judas, ¿Traidor o Héroe?, El Vocero, San Juan, Puerto Rico, Tuesday April 11 2006.

Haskel, Roberto. El Codigo Da Vinci, análisis y Bases Históricas, robhaskell@gmail.com.

Haskell, Roberto. El Evangelio Perdido de Judas, robhaskell@gmail.com.

Marcano Montañés, Jaime. Las Profecias Sobre El Nuevo Papa, El Vocero, San Juan, Puerto Rico, Thursday April 21 2005.

www.conpoder.com/simbolos

www.tripod.com/billg/Egipto/simbolos

www.geocities.com/mentirag12/pg6

www.puntarenas.com/carnavales/historia

www.logon.org

www.ccg.org

Made in the USA
Columbia, SC
11 May 2021